Titan Clash

Sigmund Brouwer

orca sports

ORCA BOOK PUBLISHERS

Library and Archives Canada Cataloguing in Publication

Brouwer, Sigmund, 1959-
Titan clash / written by Sigmund Brouwer.
(Orca sports)
ISBN 978-1-55143-721-7
1. Basketball--Juvenile fiction. I. Title. II. Series.

PS8553.R68467T57 2007   jC813'.54   C2006-907045-8

First published in the United States, 2007
Library of Congress Control Number: 2006940591

Summary: Jack is on track for a college basketball scholarship,
but his world starts to crumble when his mother has
a car accident and his father is arrested for fraud.

Orca Book Publishers gratefully acknowledges the support for its publishing
programs provided by the following agencies: the Government of Canada
through the Book Publishing Industry Development Program and the Canada
Council for the Arts, and the Province of British Columbia through the BC Arts
Council and the Book Publishing Tax Credit.

Cover design by Doug McCaffry
Cover photography by Getty Images
Author photo by Bill Bilsley

ORCA BOOK PUBLISHERS
PO Box 5626, STN. B
VICTORIA, BC Canada
V8R 6S4

ORCA BOOK PUBLISHERS
PO Box 468
CUSTER, WA USA
98240-0468

www.orcabook.com
Printed and bound in Canada.
Printed on 100% PCW recycled paper.

13 12 11 10 • 6 5 4 3

chapter one

I couldn't tell whether the crowd in the gym was more excited about the basketball game or the chance to win a free pickup truck.

I mean, Turner, Indiana, is definitely crazy about high school basketball. Our town has 7,954 people. And on this Saturday afternoon, like all game days, it seemed as if 7,950 of them had turned out to watch the season-opening game of the Turner High Titans. Stores and service stations had shut down for the afternoon. The babies, kids, parents and old people—even grumpy Mr. Broadworth in his wheelchair—made for one huge screaming crowd.

I knew one person was definitely missing: Mom; she was in the hospital. And two other people I knew were absent were the Gould brothers, in jail for unpaid speeding tickets. But to give you an idea of how big high school basketball is in Turner, Sheriff Mackenzie had come to the game. He left the Gould brothers behind with a radio to listen to the play-by-play broadcast.

And if that weren't enough to fill the gym, there were another six hundred fans for the Wolford Wolves, our opponents, from a high school fifteen miles away. The high school band, the cheerleaders, and the television and radio crews added to the chaos.

Along with one hundred and fifty gray pigeons. And one unusual-looking brown pigeon.

Yes, pigeons. Around here, pigeons are a lot cheaper than doves. One hundred and fifty-one pigeons sat onstage in a large cage in front of the school band. They were about to be released as part of a promotion for Turner Chev Olds, the local car dealership where my dad worked as head accountant.

I could see Dad from where I stood with the other players near the bench at the side of the court.

Dad stood on the stage beside the pigeon cage with a man named Ike Bothwell. Ike and his brother, Ted, owned Turner Chev Olds. Ted wasn't here—he never showed up for anything fun.

Ike held a microphone, waiting for the ra-pa-pum marching band music to end. Seeing Dad and Ike together, I found it hard to believe they had been best friends since high school.

Dad, with his dark hair and long lean face looked like Abe Lincoln without a beard. Dad wore what he always did—white shirt, black pants, black suspenders and a narrow black tie.

Ike, with his usual unlit cigar in his left hand, was anything but tall and thin. His big black cowboy hat covered his bald head. His wide belly oozed over his belt like volcano lava hanging over the edge of a cliff. Ike's checkered shirt, blue jeans and cowboy boots were his trademark. He always wore them during his late-night television commercials, where he lit a big cigar and told folks to "Come on down to Turner Chev Olds for the best old-fashioned deals in the state!" Except, Turner Chev Olds was losing money. I knew that from Dad. And that was the reason for the pigeons.

Losing money or not, Ike was putting on a good face for the public. He grinned and tapped his feet to the band's music.

Dad just stood there with his arms crossed. He didn't like the pigeon promotion idea. Even if he had liked it, his face would look set in stone.

Ike was crazy about the idea. He, of course, had thought it up.

The odd-looking brown pigeon had a little capsule attached to its leg by a tiny band of paper. Inside the capsule was a coupon that let whoever found it choose a brand-new pickup truck—for free. The way it was supposed to work was this: When the paper eventually tore, the capsule would fall from the pigeon's leg. If someone found the capsule, they'd get a truck.

That was the key word: If.

Two days earlier, when we'd talked about the pigeons, Ike had laughed a big belly laugh and told me there was very little chance anyone would find the capsule. It could end up anywhere in the county—in a lake, a garbage dump, a pile of weeds, a rain gutter. The whole point, Ike had said, still laughing, was the free publicity the car dealership would get from the event.

By the look of the crowd in the gym, his publicity plan was working. Television crews had their cameras all around. The slick Hollywood-type six o'clock newscaster from Fort Wayne's biggest station—a hundred miles away—had positioned himself right in front of the stage.

Everything was set. All that remained to be done was to release the pigeons—after opening the double doors at the end of the gym, so the pigeons could fly into the cloudless windy day outside. Then the basketball game would begin, which was all I really cared about.

The rest of the guys on the Titans felt the same way. Looking down the line of blue uniforms, I could see that my teammates were restless. Some guys bobbed up and down on their toes. Others slapped their hands against their thighs. A couple of them glanced at the scoreboard and the huge 00–00 spelled out in tiny lightbulbs.

Finally the music stopped with a few feeble wheezes from the trombones.

Ike tapped the microphone. It squealed out some noise.

He coughed into it to get our attention.

"Folks!" he shouted. His voice was so loud several people winced. Ike, I guess, didn't get the concept of a speaker system. "It's time for the big kickoff of our biggest sales event of the year! Come on down to Turner Chev Olds for the best old-fashioned deals in the great state of Indiana! Zero down and a couple of hundred a month gets you a brand-new car!"

"Just let 'em go, Ike!" someone shouted from the crowd. "Let 'em go!"

"Yeah, Ike!" someone else shouted. "I want that free truck!"

So did everybody else in town. Including my best friend, Tom Sawyer. Yes. Tom Sawyer. People bug him about his name all the time. The trouble is, he lives up to the name of Mark Twain's famous character.

I was worried about Tom.

This morning he had told me he had a plan to win the free truck, but he wouldn't give me any details. I hadn't seen Tom in the gym. I was half afraid he was waiting outside with a shotgun, ready to shoot the pigeons as they flew through the double doors.

"Folks!" Ike Bothwell shouted again into the squealing microphone. "You ask, and Turner Chev Olds delivers. Will someone at the back please open the gym doors?"

The school janitor pushed them open. The wide-open space made a hole of bright light against the fluorescent light inside the gym.

Ike looked back at the high school band. The drummer nodded and started a long theatrical drumroll.

Ike bowed, turned and opened the cage door.

Nothing happened.

Those pigeons stayed where they were.

Ike looked at the crowd watching him and grinned stupidly.

Still, the pigeons stayed inside the cage.

Ike shrugged and walked around to the back of the cage.

He waved his arms, trying to shoo them out.

The pigeons didn't budge.

Ike took off his hat and waved it. Still, the pigeons stayed in the cage.

Finally, Ike kicked at the back of the cage. It began to fall forward.

He yelped, hooked his fingers around the bars of the cage and was pulled down with it.

It fell, door down, with a loud bang. The pigeons inside finally began to flap around, but they were trapped. Feathers flew everywhere, but the birds had no place to go.

Dad rolled his eyes. It was the only sign of emotion he ever showed. He does it with me when I've done something he doesn't like. Which is often.

Dad walked over and lifted Ike off the cage. Then, with the help of two trombone players, Dad got the cage upright.

This time the pigeons made a beeline out the cage door. In a whirring explosion of gray, they burst into the gym and flew toward the open doors and daylight at the other end.

And just as suddenly as the pigeons had exploded from the cage, my friend Tom Sawyer stepped into the doorway at the end of the gym. Armed with a giant butterfly net.

chapter two

In a flash, I understood Tom's plan. He wasn't going to shoot the brown pigeon with the capsule tied to its leg. He was going to try to catch it.

Except his plan didn't quite work.

The pigeons, already scared by the falling cage, saw his dark outline in the light of the doorway. As one, they veered away from the open doors and back toward us.

Then they scattered in all directions, frantic to find safety somewhere. But there was no place to land among the lights that hung from the gym ceiling. And there was no place to land among all the screaming, waving fans.

Pigeons ducked and flew in all directions, like a swarm of oversized moths beating their wings around a porch light at night.

I guess birds try to drop weight when they're scared and flying away from danger. And there is one way for them to lose some weight quickly. With no warning, it began to rain.

But it didn't rain water.

I saw it on the news later that night. I guess the shot was too good for the television station to resist. Their Hollywood-handsome newscaster might have been the first one to get hit.

A big white smear landed on his nose and splattered his cheeks. He touched it with his fingers and stared at the mess with disbelief.

Old Mr. Broadworth was another early victim. I looked his way just as it happened. Sitting in his wheelchair, he leaned his head back to watch the pigeons above him. When he tilted his head back, his mouth opened. One second he was looking up. The next second he was gagging and spitting and reaching into his pocket for his handkerchief.

Within minutes, dozens of people had been bombed. There were squeaks and squeals and groans and outraged shouts.

I checked the stage to see what Dad was doing.

Ike, whose hat had fallen off when he'd knocked over the pigeon cage, had two white splats on his bowling-ball scalp. His eyes were as wide as if he had just swallowed a bug.

But Dad merely stood quietly with his arms still crossed and no expression on his face.

As I watched, a pigeon bombed him too, getting him squarely on the top of his head.

Dad didn't flinch. Dad didn't move. He didn't even shake his head in disgust. If I hadn't seen him take a hit to the head, I would never have guessed it had happened. Of course, he might have had the same reaction if the NBA had just drafted me. Dad's not very excitable.

I turned my eyes back to the chaos.

In the fifteen minutes it took to clear the gym, Tom Sawyer disappeared and the pigeons made the gym floor look like someone had taken a paintbrush and flicked white paint in every direction.

It took another twenty minutes for the floor to be cleaned and the lineups at the bathroom to shorten as people waited their turn to wipe themselves off.

Finally the game started.

What a way to start a season.

chapter three

I couldn't have known that night might be the peak of my season. Looking back on that first game, my guess would have been the opposite: that the season had a lot of promise.

After all, this was my senior year. I wanted to play well and have a chance at a basketball scholarship. To me, every game was as important as a play-off game.

I start at center. If I were a scout reporting on my game, I would say I'm not the slowest player, but I'm not the fastest either. I'm not taller than a lot of other players, nor a lot shorter. One of my strengths is also a weakness: My emotions stay even. I don't get upset easily, but sometimes I don't allow myself to take advantage of momentum. Another weakness is that I'm not fast at running straight ahead. But I can make up for that because I have quick hands and I study the NBA pros to copy some of their moves.

From the opening tip-off, I was smoking hot. Even if I had to say so myself, instead of hearing it from someone else, like, say, my dad. He generally focuses on my mistakes, "to help me play better next game." This time, though, I read it in the newspaper the next day.

The article said I was a "significant factor" at both ends of the court. My jump shots seemed to zero in on the net. I always seemed to be in the right spot beneath the basket to snag rebounds.

The game was going so well that early into the fourth quarter we were up 74-71, and I had scored thirty points.

The crowd got crazier and crazier as the minutes ticked by. I hit two more jumpers and scored another four points at the free-throw line. I was in a zone of concentration where everything felt like it should drop with hardly more than a swish of the net.

Every time I touched the ball, the cheering got louder and louder. I couldn't figure it out.

With five minutes left in the game, our team was up 87-86.

Finally Chuck Murray, a guard, pounded me on the back and yelled, "You're just four points away from the record!"

I must have looked as surprised as I felt because he asked, "Didn't you hear the announcer?"

I shook my head, sweat dripping onto the floor at my feet. "No. I was just thinking basketball."

He grinned. "Well, keep thinking it. You've almost got the record for the most points scored in a single game. But the game's not over, and we need you to knock down a couple more buckets."

But thoughts of the record threw off my concentration. My next shot didn't even hit the backboard.

There were three minutes left in the game. The Wolves scored coming back up the court, putting them ahead by one point.

Chuck fired a bounce pass to me. This time I managed to get my mind off the record and back on the game. From the top of the circle, I nailed another basket.

That put us back up 89–88.

But our defense couldn't stop them, and the Wolves answered with another basket. Down 89 to their 90 with less than a minute in the game.

All I was thinking was win.

We crossed the half-court line, firing passes around the perimeter. With ten seconds left on the clock, I got the ball.

The crowd screamed for me to shoot.

Nine seconds remained.

I couldn't shoot. Not with the game on the line and tight coverage from a guy who seemed twice my height.

Eight seconds.

I decided to try a new move I'd been working on.

Because I'm right-handed, I began by dribbling the ball to my left, knowing my defender was likely to go for my fake because I would be taking it back to his stronger hand. I half spun and kept dribbling, keeping my body between me and the defender.

Seven seconds.

Now for the fake spin.

I looked over my left shoulder, turning my body slightly as if I would be going that direction.

That's all it took. A subtle small move.

By instinct the defender slid back to block my spin to the net. He only took a half step in that direction. But it was enough. I made my move in the opposite direction and drove to the basket, spinning the ball off my fingertips to the net.

It hit the rim, rolled for what seemed like two hours, and then wobbled through.

Two seconds later, the buzzer sounded.

Titans, 91. Wolves, 90.

Our victory. My single-game scoring record.

I looked for Dad in the stands among the yelling, cheering fans. He gave me a short nod. Then all I saw was his back as he walked toward the gym doors.

chapter four

At twenty minutes after eleven the following Monday morning, I thought I heard my name over the school intercom.

But I wasn't sure if I had heard correctly because I was in the middle of a physics problem I had been trying to figure out for fifteen minutes. It was something about a cannonball that had been shot upward at an angle of forty-five degrees with an initial speed of one hundred miles an hour. Like how was it going to help me in life to know how long that cannonball would stay in the air and how far it would go before it landed?

I looked around. I had never been called to the office before. Sure enough, kids were looking back at me. So I must have heard right.

"Hey, Jack," one of the guys hooted from the back, "you're busted!"

I gathered my books in a pile and threw them in my backpack.

"That's right," I said. "Big bank robbery this weekend. How'd they know it was me?"

I got a few laughs, which made me feel better. See, at my height and skinniness, I definitely don't look cool. Especially after my face has lost its battle to a weekly zit attack. There are days when I wonder if having the ability to play first-string center on the team is worth the price of a geeky-looking body.

Even Mr. Jonathan smiled at my joke. He's our physics teacher, a little guy with a receding hairline and a gardening hobby. Which is definitely not cool.

"If you don't make it back to class," he told me as I reached the doorway, "be sure to have the final three problems solved and ready to turn in by tomorrow."

"Yes, sir," I said, "flying cannonballs have always fascinated me."

Laughter followed me down the hall.

It didn't occur to me to worry about why I had been called to the principal's office. I hoped it might have something to do with basketball or a scholarship or something like that.

Of course when I walked into the office, I knew it was about something else.

My first clue was finding Tom Sawyer sitting in a chair across from the secretary's desk.

The second clue was the toilet seat stuck to his hand.

Yes. A toilet seat.

chapter five

Most people with a toilet seat stuck to their hand would have looked embarrassed.

Not Tom, Mr. Freckles with the aw-shucks grin. Tom gets away with just about everything because he's so funny and because he never really means to cause harm. Like the net thing with the pigeons. He had explained himself by pointing out that there was no rule against trying to catch the pigeon. He'd made so much sense that several people said they wished they had thought of the same thing.

"Hey, Jack," he said to me. Tom had reddish-brown hair to match his freckles. He wore jeans, canvas high-top running shoes and an Indiana Pacers sweatshirt. As he spoke—with his usual grin—he was tipping back in his chair. The toilet seat rested on the chair beside him. His right arm was stretched across to the toilet seat. "I'd shake hands, man, but my glove is a little big."

He lifted his right arm slightly and wiggled the toilet seat. His entire palm was stuck to the top of it.

I groaned. Everyone knew Tom and I were close buddies. Tom was waiting in the principal's office. I had been called down. There was an obvious conclusion. "Black doesn't think I had anything to do with that, does he?" I asked, pointing at the toilet seat.

The school secretary coughed. She was about fifty years past retirement age, which made it even more of a joke that her hair was badly dyed mouse brown. Her face was as square as her body. And her faded flower-print dress was as old-fashioned as her name, which a little sign on her desk proclaimed was Enid Humphrey.

She cleared her throat with meaning, since I hadn't picked up on her cough.

"That's *Mr.* Black, young man," she said to me in her ancient raspy voice. Nothing on her bulldog face showed that she was amused by or interested in Tom and his toilet seat. "And no, you have nothing to do with your friend's problem. Mr. Black will speak with each of you separately when he gets off the telephone."

I eased myself into the chair to the left of Tom. From where we sat, we could see the closed door to Mr. Black's office. The blinds on his window that overlooked the waiting area were closed too.

Neither of us said anything for several moments. I was waiting for Tom to explain the toilet seat. Maybe he was waiting for me to ask.

So I finally did. "Okay, how did it happen? And why?"

"Krazy Glue," he said. "You know, that super glue that sticks anything together."

"Krazy Glue," I repeated. "You decided to glue your hand to a toilet seat."

"No," he said. "I decided to glue Mad Max to a toilet seat."

Mad Max is what we call our industrial arts teacher. Mr. Max has been known to yell at students and kick apart their projects on occasion.

"See," Tom said, "there's this kid in class with an allergy problem. He kept sneezing and Mad Max went nuts on him for interrupting. Mad Max threatened to take a hammer to the kid's birdhouse, and it made him cry. So I figured..."

I nodded. In the back wing of the school, by the industrial arts shop, there is a staff rest room. Max is the only teacher in that wing—which is why he gets away with yelling and breaking projects—and would be the only teacher to use that restroom.

"Anyway," Tom said, "everyone knows that Mad Max always takes an eleven o'clock break. I started working on the toilet seat at about a quarter to."

"Working on it?" I said. I noticed Enid Humphrey was listening closely, although she was trying to pretend she wasn't.

"Yeah," Tom said, "it was a genius plan. I loosened the toilet seat bolts before I added the glue. That way when he finished using it and stood up, the seat would stick to...well, you know. I thought it would be hilarious to see him hopping around trying to unstick himself."

Did I see a smile start to crack Enid Humphrey's face?

"What went wrong?" I asked.

"My conscience," Tom said sadly. "You know how I sometimes do things without thinking."

"Really," I said sarcastically. Tom's family lives two blocks from mine. I've known him since kindergarten. On the first day I met him, he had tried to stand on his bicycle seat on a downhill run. I'd even gone with him to the hospital where we both cared more about the lollipops the nurses gave us than the stitches he got on his elbow.

"Really," he said, missing my sarcasm. "I had to time it perfectly so the glue wouldn't dry before he got there. So I waited until just before eleven. I had just finished spreading the last of the Krazy Glue when it hit me that maybe what I was doing was a little too much. Even to play a joke on Mad Max. So I grabbed a paper towel to wipe off the seat, but because it was so close to eleven, I was in too much of a hurry. I made the mistake of leaning on the seat with one hand as I reached to wipe with the other. And, of course, I leaned on a big spot of Krazy Glue."

Tom pointed with his left hand at the right hand stuck to the seat. He grinned. "But it wasn't a complete waste. You should have seen the look on Mad Max's face when he saw me with this thing stuck to my hand."

"Look," I said, "when Black—"

I heard another cough from Enid Humphrey.

"When Mr. Black asks you about this," I continued, "make sure you tell him how Mad Max goes nuts in class. It probably won't get you out of trouble, but maybe someone official will finally do something about him."

Probably not, though. Mad Max is only a couple of years away from retiring. He hasn't ever really harmed anyone, and I guessed it would be easier for the school board to ignore him until he retired. At least that was the way Dad had explained it to me once.

"Sounds like a good idea," Tom said. He frowned. "What did you get called down here for?"

"I don't know," I answered.

As if in response to Tom's question, Mr. Black opened his office door. He was older, with white hair and a white goatee. He wore a dark blue suit and walked with a cane.

Mr. Black didn't come out of his office; he just stood in the doorway. He looked at us, back and forth a few times, maybe deciding who to call first. He shook his head sadly at Tom, then moved his eyes to me again.

"Jack," he said, "step into my office."

I nodded and stood, suddenly worried.

Mr. Black's voice had sounded a little too serious for my liking.

chapter six

Mr. Black shut the door behind me, pointed to a chair in front of his desk and sat down at his desk. It was cluttered with stacks of papers. A coffee mug had left a wet ring on the right side of the desk. On the left, a small statue of the Eiffel Tower held down a pile of papers. The statue was a souvenir from a trip he had taken to Paris with a group of high school students last year. I had been one of those students. A small plaque at the bottom read *To Monsieur Black, the best of the best.*

Although I knew what the plaque said, I read it again because I was nervous and I wanted some place to look other than at Mr. Black.

It didn't help that he sighed a heavy sigh. Then another.

I finally looked up at him.

He ran his fingers through his hair and took another deep breath.

This was getting worse and worse. What could be so bad that even he didn't want to discuss it?

He inhaled deeply through his nose. He opened his mouth to say something. Then he shut his mouth again.

I waited, only because I didn't know what else to do.

He shook his head slowly from side to side. "That Tom Sawyer," he finally said. "Can you believe what he did this time?"

"Um, yes sir," I answered. After all, I knew Tom.

"I guess I can too," he said. "I'll miss him when he graduates. Life is always interesting with him around."

"Yes, sir," I said. I didn't think this was why he had called me into his office.

I waited some more.

Mr. Black opened his mouth again. And closed it again. He sighed once more, and then he ran his fingers through his hair.

"Jack," he said slowly, "I wanted you to hear this from me, so you can prepare yourself. Because in a town this small, you won't be able to hide it from anyone. And believe me, people will talk."

"Talk?" I echoed.

"Let me be the first to say that there has to be a good explanation," Mr. Black continued, staring at the Eiffel Tower on his desk. "I mean, if he did it, he must have had a good reason."

"Talk?" I said again.

Mr. Black lifted his head and looked me square in the eyes. "And even if he didn't have a good reason, you shouldn't think any less of him. Everyone makes mistakes.

He's a good man. Whatever happens, don't forget that."

"Who's a good man?" I asked. If Mr. Black was trying to make this easier on me—whatever this was—he was doing a terrible job.

"Jack..." Mr. Black paused. He closed his eyes for a moment, and then he tried again. "Let me say that I can't even believe it myself."

"Can't believe what?" I asked. I was starting to really get worried.

"I consider you a friend," he said. "We got to know each other on the school trip to Paris. I know you're a smart young man with a bright future ahead of you. You must not let this—"

"Sir," I interrupted, "can you just tell me what's going on?"

He blinked a few times. He looked at the ceiling. He looked at his desk. He looked past my shoulder and out the window.

"It's your father," he finally said quietly. "He's been arrested."

I laughed. I guess I surprised Mr. Black, because he snapped his eyes right back to mine.

"You had me worried," I explained. "The way you were drawing this out."

"You expected this?" Mr. Black asked.

"No," I said. "Of course not. It's just that there is no way in the world my dad would do anything illegal. Unless it's against the law to follow rules and regulations. He's the last person in the world who would get in real trouble. I mean, if his dentist told him to brush his teeth with fifty strokes on each side, he would count those strokes as he brushed and make sure he did exactly fifty. So if Dad's been arrested, it's either a joke or a mistake."

"Fraud," Mr. Black said. "The charges against him are fraud and embezzlement. Half a million dollars are missing from the business accounts of Turner Chev Olds. People are already guessing he was desperate because of your mom's hospital bills."

My smile faded. Two weeks earlier, Mom had driven around a blind corner and almost hit a kid on a bike. She couldn't stop the car quickly enough and had swerved off the road to avoid him. And she had hit a tree—hard.

She had broken a number of bones and had spent almost fourteen hours on the operating table. Our insurance only covered half of the huge medical bills.

"Ike Bothwell himself called me, so I could tell you before everyone started talking," Mr. Black said. "As head accountant, your dad was in a position to take the money, and Ted Bothwell tracked him through the accounting files."

My dad stole half a million dollars? My dad, who grilled me every day on how much I should value my reputation? My strict dad, who made me come home early every night to keep me out of trouble? My rule-following dad, who...

"I'm sorry," Mr. Black said, understanding the confusion on my face. "The state police have taken him up to South Bend. Chances are he'll be out on bail in a couple of days. Until then, you should be able to visit him."

"I see," I said, not seeing at all.

Mr. Black stood up. "If I were you, I wouldn't try to avoid this. If people ask you about it, tell them it's true—the arrest part, at least. Tell them to wait until all the facts come out before they make any judgments."

I stood up too.

As he showed me to the door, Mr. Black stopped and put his hand on my shoulder.

"The sad thing," he said, "is that plenty of people are going to jump to conclusions. It's human nature. They'll be happy to have someone else's trouble to worry about. Just remember that, all right? Because your next few days aren't going to be easy at all. And if I can help in any way, let me know."

All I could do was nod. I didn't trust my voice.

Dad was arrested for stealing half a million dollars from his best friend?

This was horrible.

I wished I'd just had a toilet seat stuck to my hand.

chapter seven

It didn't take long for people to hear about Dad.

At practice that afternoon, some of the guys wouldn't even look me in the eye. As we gathered around Coach Buckley, the air seemed charged, as if he had just spent five minutes yelling at us for slacking off. It was like there was a bag of smelly garbage in the corner of the gym that everyone tried to pretend wasn't there.

And what was I going to do? Bring it up myself? I mean, my dad was in jail. I didn't want to think about it. Not until I had to, which would happen after practice when I drove up to South Bend to see him.

Things got better when we finished our drills and split up for a series of three-on-three scrimmages. Everyone concentrated so much on basketball that nothing else was a distraction.

Bill Davis, a short fast kid with a deadly shot, Chuck Murray and I went up against three freshmen—Ronnie Smith, Jarvis Marlow and Tim Carleton.

The fun thing about playing freshmen is that you have a couple of years on them and you can try some things you might not try against more experienced players. The not-so-fun thing is they have nothing to lose. Since everyone expected us to beat them, the win wouldn't matter. But if they somehow managed to beat us, we would get razzed mercilessly. And with something to prove, freshmen always played extra hard against older players.

Coach Buckley's way of setting up three-on-threes is to give us five minutes. He acts as referee, calling only the most obvious fouls. The rest of the guys on the team stand on the sidelines to cheer or jeer, depending on how the game goes.

Coach is a big dark-haired guy who always wears a blue shiny nylon tracksuit, which he's had since the 1970s. Unfortunately for Coach Buckley, the tracksuit has not grown along with him. He fills it tight, like a water balloon. And, because of his size, he can't move too fast.

He waddled to the center of the court, his whistle swinging like a pendulum from his neck. As he got ready to toss the ball to start the scrimmage, the gym door opened.

My stomach turned to a heavy rock as I recognized the man in the doorway: Ted Bothwell, Ike's brother.

Ted walked into the gym, not caring that all eyes were on him. He wore his usual suit and tie, his dark hair combed straight back.

Was he here for me? Had he come about my dad?

Coach Buckley waved one of the players over from the sidelines and gave him the whistle and the ball.

"Take over," Coach said. Then he walked off the court to talk to Ted.

And our mini-game began.

I was rattled by the sight of Ted Bothwell and worried about the reason for his visit. That's my excuse. Halfway into the five minutes, we were down by a basket to the freshmen; normally we would have been up by at least eight points.

Our opponents could sense a possible win, and they played even harder.

The guys on the sidelines egged them on, jeering at us seniors.

We scored two baskets to give us a lead, but with a minute left, and the score so close, even if we won, it would seem like a loss.

I had to focus. I finally managed to stop thinking about Ted Bothwell and my dad.

I called for the ball.

What we needed to regain some pride was a move that would stun the freshmen. A move that would make the guys on the sidelines turn to one another in astonishment.

And I knew who I wanted to try it against: Tim Carleton. He had scored the most against us. He was the cockiest freshman. He was the one with the biggest grin. He was the one who most wanted to be the hero. And he was the one guarding me.

At the top of the circle, I dribbled between my legs. Then through them again.

I faked a drive toward the baseline and pulled up as Carleton swiped at the ball. I bobbed my shoulders one way, then another, trying to play loosey-goosey, making it look like every part of my body was heading a different direction.

When I went up for my shot, I was wide open—Carleton had dived to the spot where it looked like I was headed. I double-pumped as one of the other freshmen leaped to block me, and I hit a soft shot as I faded back to the hardwood.

Swoosh.

Nothing but net as two of the freshmen went sliding across the floor, while the third freshman just stared.

For a second, there was a wonderful stunned silence on the sidelines.

Then, after that brief pause, came the whistles and shouts of glee.

The rest of the scrimmage went totally our way. We finished with a ten-point lead.

I would have stopped to enjoy our win if not for one thing.

As the next three-on-three started, Coach Buckley called me over to talk to Ted Bothwell.

I grabbed a towel and wiped the sweat off my face and arms as I walked over to them.

"Yes, sir," I said, half expecting Coach to yell at me.

"You know the situation with your father," Ted Bothwell said matter-of-factly.

"He didn't do anything wrong," I said.

"That is very loyal of you, son. But I'm not here to find him guilty of anything. That is up to the legal system."

"He didn't do anything wrong," I repeated.

Ted Bothwell smiled, briefly showing his white, white teeth. "I'm glad you feel that way. Perhaps you'll be willing to help me then."

"Sir?"

"Did your father give you anything in the last week?" he asked. "Anything that he wanted you to keep safe for him?"

"No," I answered, wondering what he was talking about.

Ted Bothwell looked at me earnestly and put his hands on my shoulders. His palms contacted my sweat, though, and he pulled his hands away. He didn't do a very good job of hiding the distaste he felt.

"Jack," Ted said after a moment, "it is very important that you not lie to me about this. I imagine when he gave it to you, he told you to keep it a secret. But if you know he is innocent, you can tell me where you put it."

"He didn't give me anything," I said. "I don't know what you're talking about. My dad is not a liar and neither am I."

"All right then," he answered. "That's all I wanted to ask you."

He turned his attention to Coach Buckley. I had been dismissed as if I were a six-year-old.

They spoke for another ten minutes, just the two of them, huddled by the bottom of the bleachers.

And I was miserable for the rest of practice. All I could think about was my dad, in jail.

chapter eight

Most people don't think much about jail, especially when they're from Turner, Indiana. Sure, our little town has a sheriff's office. Not because Turner is so big, but because it's the biggest town for ten or fifteen miles in any direction. Our jail, though, is just a cell in the back of the sheriff's office. More often than not, Sheriff Mackenzie leaves the cell unlocked because his "prisoners" are just there to sleep off a night of too much alcohol. Our town, in fact, feels a lot like Mayberry, from the old *Andy Griffith Show*. And the jail looks a lot like the one in those black-and-white reruns.

So when I walked into the building where my dad was being held in South Bend, I was not prepared for what I saw. Or heard. Or smelled.

Sweat and old cigarette smoke and other body odors blasted my nose. From cells beyond the main doors, I heard yelling and moaning and, every once in a while, a high-pitched crazy laughing. The walls were dull white, pocked by cigarette burns and scratched with graffiti. It was a place of no hope.

I sat in the visitors' area, waiting for someone to bring Dad out to see me. I could still hardly believe any of this was really happening. After practice, I had stopped briefly to see Mom in the hospital. Then I had made the hour-long drive to South Bend in the used Camaro I had bought early in the year from Ike's dealership. Ike had given me an unbelievably low price—because Ike and Dad were such good friends, and because I worked at the dealership during the summers. While I drove, I had been too depressed to even listen to music. Dad? In jail? And here I was, driving a car that was nearly given to me by the guy Dad was accused of stealing from.

My depression, of course, only got worse as I waited.

Finally the door at the far end of the room opened. A guard brought Dad through. The door shut behind them with an awful solid sound.

Dad wore a bright orange jumpsuit like all the other prisoners. His face was smeared with grime. But worst of all, his hands were cuffed together in front of him.

I felt like throwing up.

Dad shuffled toward me, head down.

The guard pointed him toward a chair across the table from me. Then the guard walked over and leaned against the far wall. He lit a cigarette. Dad and I would not be alone as we talked.

Dad lifted his head and looked at me.

"How was the drive?" he asked. "No speeding tickets, right?"

He always made sure I drove the speed limit. He threatened to take away my driving privileges if I got a ticket. I wondered if he realized how funny it was that he was asking these questions from jail. But I didn't point that out.

"No speeding tickets," I answered.

"How is Mom taking this?" he asked.

"You didn't call her?" I said in surprise.

"I tried," Dad answered. "But the nurse said she was asleep. I didn't want to wake her. Not for this news. And it's not like I can call back whenever I want."

"When I stopped by the hospital she was knocked out on painkillers," I said. "So I just held her hand for a while."

"Maybe that's just as well," he said.

A silence hung between us. A silence where we both thought about why Dad couldn't call Mom. Because he was in jail.

"How long are they going to keep you here?" I finally asked.

"I've hired a South Bend lawyer because Mr. Rondell represents Ike and Turner Chev Olds."

I understood. Mr. Rondell was Turner's only lawyer. In something like this, Mr. Rondell couldn't work for Ike and for Dad.

"Anyway," Dad said, "this lawyer says I'll have to stay until tomorrow. That's when I get a hearing in front of a judge, who will set bail. After we post bail, I can come home again."

"Oh," I said.

Another silence hung between us.

I had heard the phrase "post bail" plenty of times on television, on cop shows and on lawyer shows. I knew what it meant. Basically a security deposit had to be paid. If Dad didn't show up for his trial date, he would lose the deposit.

This time, Dad broke the silence.

"You haven't asked me whether I took the money," he said.

"I didn't think I needed to ask," I said.

Dad reached his cuffed hands across the table and squeezed my hand. "Thanks," he said.

That's when I realized exactly how tough this was on him. I mean, I imagine when I was little he would have picked me up or hugged me. But these days he barely even pats me on the shoulder. Being a man, he always says, means acting like a man. And that, he always says, means standing on your own. So he's let me learn how to deal with my own cuts and scrapes and disappointments.

"Time's up," the guard called.

Dad stood up, and the guard led him back into the hallway that led to the cells and the noises and the smells no one should have to face for a night.

I wanted to cry, for Dad and for myself. Because there was one thing louder than anything Dad had said. It was what he had not said.

Dad had not told me he was innocent.

chapter nine

I got back to Turner at about nine o'clock. Somehow the tree-lined streets seemed different. Tall elms still rose gracefully on each side. But I no longer had a sense of old-fashioned small-town peace in seeing the trees that had been growing since before World War II.

And when I turned onto our driveway, the house in the glow of my car headlights seemed different too. It was still a two-story, country-style house with yellow paint, white trim and a wide porch. But it no longer seemed like home.

I turned the motor off and sat behind the steering wheel with my window partly rolled down. It was so quiet I could clearly hear the ticking of the car's engine as it cooled down.

Why do things seem so different? I wondered.

I realized after a while that the town and my house had not changed. I had. I had spent my life among neighbors and friends in Turner who knew me as well as I knew them. But I no longer felt like I could walk around town without being stared at. I felt like a freak because my dad had been arrested.

Home has always been the one place I felt secure, no matter how bad things were at school or on the basketball court. But it no longer seemed like a safe place where my dad was a giant rock of stability. I could always trust him, even when his rules and regulations and strictness drove me nuts or bored me to death.

It made me sad to realize that my home had been taken away from me in a small way.

I sat there for a few more minutes. Then I told myself to quit feeling sorry for myself. I took a deep breath and went into the house.

At seventeen, I'm old enough to spend the night alone. Especially in Turner, where help is as easy to get as shouting.

Inside the house, I hung up my coat, something I never seem to remember to do when Dad's there. I put the newspaper in the magazine rack instead of leaving it on the front porch. As I straightened, I noticed the light blinking on the answering machine.

Three messages.

The first was a message from Ike Bothwell, asking me to call him no matter how late I got in.

The second was from Tom, telling me he felt bad about what had happened and that he was sure there was a mistake and that there was no way my dad could have done what people said he had.

And then there was the third message. I had to play it twice to make sure I heard it correctly. Both times the harsh whisper of the caller sent goose bumps in waves across my scalp.

"The wages of sin is death," the voice rasped. "And the punishment of the sinner will be inflicted unto the second and third generations. The snake of evil will be crushed and killed."

That was it. The creepy voice could have been a man or a woman, young or old.

Now my home seemed even stranger to me.

I waited five minutes to call Ike Bothwell. It took me that long to get up the courage.

"Jack," he answered without waiting for me to tell him who I was.

My silence told him he had surprised me.

"I've got a caller ID phone," he said. "It showed the Spencer number. And you're the only one who would be there tonight."

Yeah, I thought, because Mom is in the hospital. And Dad is in jail.

I kept my thoughts to myself.

"Anyway," he said, "I'm glad you called. I want to talk to you about what's going on."

"Um, okay," I said. Although I sort of just wanted to hang up.

"Good. When can you get here?"

"Well," I said, "I've got basketball practice after school and—"

"No," he said, "I meant when can you get here tonight?"

"Tonight?"

"Yes," he said, "unless you'd rather just lie awake and wonder what I want to tell you about your dad."

It was only about nine-thirty. And Ike was right: I would lie awake and wonder what he had to say.

"I guess I'll be right over," I said.

chapter ten

Ike Bothwell and his wife, Judy, lived in a huge ranch-style house on a spread just outside of town. I knew this from all the times my family had been invited over for Sunday barbecues. That was before Mom's car accident, of course. And before Dad had been accused of stealing half a million dollars from Ike.

The Bothwells' driveway was lined with floodlights that sent arcs of white and blue light into the trees. At the end of the long driveway, I could see Ike's house and four-car garage.

Ike was waiting for me in the doorway when I got out of my Camaro. His public act of cowboy hat and checkered shirt wasn't really a public act. He wore the same clothes at home. But tonight he wasn't wearing his hat.

He invited me in.

The foyer had a tiled floor and led to a large living room with a fireplace so big you could roast a couple of cows. The floor was hardwood, with expensive area rugs. The walls were covered with large oil paintings, mainly western scenes.

Ike's wife was waiting on the couch. She gave me a tired smile as I walked toward her.

Like my dad, at first she didn't seem to suit Ike. Where Ike looked big and clumsy, she was a tiny woman and moved with the daintiness of a songbird. Where Ike looked country, she was clearly big city, with short blond hair and perfect white teeth and expensive clothing. Odd as they might look as a couple, I'd seen them together at all those Sunday barbecues, and it was easy to tell how much they loved each other.

"I'm so sad about what's happened to your dad," she said. "I hope you're doing okay."

"Yes, ma'am," I said. Kids learn fast from grown-ups. In a situation like this, you're not supposed to tell the absolute truth. You're not supposed to admit that you just listened to a really creepy message that has you a little scared. You're not supposed to say that you're worried sick about your dad spending a night in a place full of horrible smells and noises, or about your mom in the hospital. You're not supposed to say that you don't even dare think that your dad might be guilty.

"Sit," Ike said, pointing at a chair near a tray of cheese and crackers and a pitcher of lemonade. "Please sit. Judy thought you might be hungry."

I sat.

Ike poured the lemonade into a glass and handed it to me.

I was surprised by how nice they were being.

And I was surprised to discover how hungry I was. Then I remembered I hadn't really eaten since lunch.

"How's your dad?" Ike asked.

I guess my face must have shown my surprise at the concern in his voice.

"Jack," Ike said softly, "please understand. I had nothing to do with his arrest. Unless someone can convince me otherwise with hard proof, I can't believe he did it. Even with hard proof, I would still have doubts."

I nodded slowly. Ike couldn't know how much better his words made me feel.

"Dad seems all right," I said. "He told me they should let him out on bail tomorrow."

"I'm angry that he has to spend any time in jail," Judy said. "It should never have happened this way. Ted had no right taking this to the state police until we had a chance to—"

"That's enough," Ike said mildly. "Poor Jack here doesn't need to get sucked into a family battle."

Not that the Bothwell family difficulties were too secret in such a small town. It was well known that Ike's brother, Ted, was the opposite of Ike. Ike was easygoing, loved having fun, and had no problem lending or giving people money. Ted was rigid—a rules and regulations guy without a heart.

Ike sighed and leaned back in his chair.

"You remember the pigeon promotion, Jack?"

"Yes?" I said slowly, wondering about the abrupt change of subject.

"Your dad fought me long and hard over it," Ike said. "And when he realized I wouldn't give in, he advised me to get insurance."

"Insurance?"

Ike nodded. "You can get special insurance to cover a stunt like that. You pay a couple of thousand dollars, and if someone wins, the insurance company covers the cost of the truck you have to give away. I told your dad no. I thought there was so little chance the capsule would be found that it wasn't worth paying a couple of thousand just to be safe."

Ike shook his head. "But now I expect your dad was right on both counts. First of all, I'll be lucky if the capsule doesn't get found. And when someone finds it, it'll cost me about twenty thousand for the truck."

He kept shaking his head. "And second, it was just a dumb idea. I got publicity, all right, but the wrong kind. It didn't help me at all that those pigeons did their little business on the heads of half the people in town."

"Don't beat yourself up," Judy said softly. "You couldn't have known that would happen."

"That's my point," Ike told her. "Jack's dad did. And I didn't listen to him."

Ike turned back to me. "And it's only gotten worse from there."

"Worse?" I echoed.

"Do you have any idea how many complaints I'm getting from animal rights people, from police, from anyone who's had pigeons land on their property?"

I shook my head.

"Let me put it this way," Ike said. "I seem to have single-handedly started open season on brown pigeons. For a fifty-mile radius, idiots with shotguns are blasting at any brown bird that looks remotely like a pigeon, hoping to bring down a brand-new pickup truck with a dead bird."

It would have been funny, I guess, if this were a cartoon where real blood and guts weren't getting splattered, where real people weren't endangered by trigger-happy hunters. That's something I don't like about television—it makes you forget that violence can have a real effect.

"Your dad told me that's exactly what would happen," Ike said. "But I told him he was a wet blanket who always looked for the worst in any situation."

Ike reached past me and scooped up a handful of cheese and crackers.

"Ike Bothwell!" Judy said. "Remember your diet."

"I remember it all right," he mumbled. "I remember how much I hate it."

He crunched a mouthful of crackers. Crumbs drifted down onto his big belly. His wife shook her head with an affectionate smile.

Ike swallowed, and then he continued, "So, Jack, my point is that your dad is not a stupid man. He thinks everything through carefully, even if it only involves pigeons. If he were going to steal half a million dollars, he would do it in such a way that he couldn't get caught. He certainly wouldn't leave a paper trail. In other words, I think he's innocent. That's one of the reasons I wanted to talk to you tonight."

"One of the reasons?" I said.

Ike frowned. "The other reason hardly makes sense."

"Don't be dramatic, Ike," Judy said. "Just tell him."

"Jack," Ike said, "I asked your dad point-blank if he stole that money. He wouldn't say yes or no. All he'd say was that your mom's car accident wasn't an accident. And that he—your dad—should have known better."

"I don't get it," I said.

"Neither did I," Ike said. "So I had a talk with Sheriff Mackenzie. He took me to the junkyard, and we had a closer look at your mom's car."

Ike's frown got bigger.

"Jack," Ike said, "it looks like someone messed with the brakes. That's why she couldn't stop in time. That's why she had to swerve off the road to miss that kid and his bike."

chapter eleven

"Hey, loser, I hear your dad's in jail."

I wasn't sure I'd heard right. I was on the gym floor, facing the center for the Brookville Barracudas. The crowd noise was high for the opening tipoff of the midweek game.

Their center—Number 15—was a little taller than I am, with a shadow of dark fuzz on his face. He curled his lips up in a sneer, showing more gums than teeth.

"So," he said in answer to my puzzled squint, "what's it like to be the son of a jailbird?"

"Why you—" I began to snarl.

The referee tossed the ball into the air. I got caught flatfooted, and Number 15 easily knocked the ball behind him to his teammate.

The crowd groaned slightly. Before I could react to not reacting, the Barracudas had moved the ball ahead, passing around me and attacking us with a full-court press. By the time I caught up to the play, they'd scored an easy bucket.

I could see frowns on some of my teammates faces. Expressions that said they had no idea what I was doing but I'd better get into the game.

We moved the ball back up the court.

Just inside their zone, I took a pass. I backed up, drawing Number 15 toward me. I kept backing up. My body moved automatically; my mind was still focused on my anger.

What Number 15 didn't know was that he'd made a mistake.

When I get mad, I don't do stupid things. Ever since I was a little kid, my dad has drilled me about keeping my temper. An outburst is the thing he puts up with the least. If I lose my temper, he finds a way to remind me not to do it again, whether it's by making me do extra chores or by grounding me. Long ago I learned to take my anger and bottle it up inside. Then I let it out slowly and use it.

"Does that make you a jailbird loser too?" Number 15 taunted me. "Did good old Dad teach you how to rip people off?"

Now that his insults weren't catching me off guard, I could keep my head in the game.

It was time to let my anger out slowly.

Although, like most basketball players, I have a bunch of moves I use in different situations, I believe a player should try to develop the Move, something that sets him apart.

Like Shaquille O'Neal. He uses his size to back in as he dribbles, ramming the defending center closer and closer to the net as he keeps the ball in front and out of reach. When Shaq is close enough, he hooks one leg around his opponent as he spins toward the hoop, at the same time bringing the ball up to slam dunk it like a sledgehammer driving a thumbtack.

Shaq's move works nearly every time. You can see it coming, but Shaq is so quick for a man so big that the other player really has no chance.

And that's the first thing about the Move. Just like Shaq's move, it has to work even after every coach in the league has warned his players about it.

The second thing? The Move has to lead to points. A center court Move doesn't mean anything to the game and is just a waste of time. Sports highlights on television never show a Move that misses the basket.

But even if the Move works nearly every time, and even if it usually leads to points, it's not the Move if it doesn't look good. If it's something big and awkward like some tall, tall guy just laying in fadeaway jumpers because no one has his reach, it doesn't count as the Move. But say someone is low-posting it and spins so quickly the defender looks like a dead elephant, and people gasp—that's the Move.

And I had one I worked hard on, every game. It was one I had seen Allen Iverson, a Philadelphia 76er, do time and again on television. It was one built for my biggest strength: quick hands.

I was ready to try it now. Number 15 was in front of me, guarding my move to the center lane.

All I did was start working toward him. I began to do crossover dribbles, switching from my right hand to my left hand to my right hand. Still slowly walking.

"Hey, yahoo," I said to Number 15, "here's the deal."

I spoke low, so only he could hear me.

"I'm going to do this to you about twenty times tonight, maybe more if I get the ball a lot."

"Do what?" He made a quick stab for the ball with his right hand. I backed up with the ball.

"Watch closely," I said. "Maybe you'll figure it out. If not, you'll have plenty of chances to learn it."

I advanced toward him again. Ball to the left hand. To the right hand. To the left hand, walking slow enough to drive him nuts. Slow enough that he lost his patience.

He committed to my left side, going for the ball on what he thought was my weaker hand. As he did, I rolled the ball over to the right, almost palming it in a quick move that left him too far forward. And just like that I was around him into the open lane. Halfway through my lay-up, I dumped the ball with a short underhand pass to Chuck Murray, who casually rose with it and pumped it into the net off the backboard.

As I jogged backward up the court, I grinned at Number 15.

"At the end of the night," I said, "let's see who's the loser."

I slowly fed off my anger all night. Every second or third time I came down the court, I announced to Number 15 that he should watch closely. That he should get ready to have his shorts tangled.

And every time, I beat him. Not always for baskets, because their coach started to send someone in to double-team me. But when I didn't have a chance at the net myself, I always found someone open.

Best of all, Number 15 began to get some of the medicine he had tried to give me to throw off my game. He began to lose his temper.

By the third quarter, we were up by twenty points. I blew past him again, and he fouled me.

I made both free throws. And then all the others as he fouled me again and again. His coach finally benched him.

We won easily. And I walked off the court with a feeling of angry satisfaction. I enjoyed keeping it inside, because with it there, I had no room for my worries.

That's why I was smiling when Coach Buckley called to me in the locker room and asked me to join him in his office. I'd played a good game, we'd won, and I felt great about finding a way to stop Number 15 without losing my temper.

My smile disappeared in a big hurry when Coach told me why he wanted to speak to me alone.

He was cutting me from the team.

chapter twelve

"Cut," I said, repeating the word. "Cut?" My mind struggled with the concept.

On the plain white walls of his office, Coach Buckley had photos of all his previous teams. Small trophies held down piles of papers on his desk. In my confusion, it was all a blur.

"Cut, like gone from the team cut?" I said.

Coach Buckley kept nodding. His eyes would not meet mine.

Outside the office, I heard the buzz of the crowd as people left the school. It was always like that. Like air slowly escaping from a balloon, the excitement level in the gym dropped as people left. Soon all that would remain was an echoing gym and the empty paper cups and other trash that littered the stands. I knew because there were times when I wandered back into the empty gym and stood there alone to think over a game.

But if I was truly gone from the team, I would never have that experience again. All my memories would be tainted.

Cut?

"Coach," I said, hardly able to speak. "Why? I mean the game I just played..."

"This has nothing to do with your ability," he said, staring at a pen on his desk.

"Then why?" I asked. "Is this some kind of bad joke? You know that if I can't play basketball, I don't have a chance at a scholarship."

I waited for him to smile and explain that it was just a bad joke.

He didn't.

"Why?" I repeated.

Coach Buckley began to shuffle some papers on his desk. "Everyone on this team is subject to the same rules and conditions. The high school charter says that—"

"High school charter?" I echoed.

"Yes," he said, irritated, "charter. The set of founding rules. This high school was built in 1914. Its founding rules state that athletes can play on school teams subject to acceptable moral behavior."

Moral behavior? Like whether a person was good or bad?

Because the biggest thing on my mind was that my dad was in jail, I guessed the coach was judging us both.

"My dad is innocent!" I said, standing and beginning to lose my temper in spite of myself. "And how dare you decide that what he's charged with has anything to do with my behavior!"

Coach Buckley kept shuffling his papers. He didn't respond. I suddenly felt stupid standing in front of him. I snapped my mouth shut and sat down again.

"It's not your dad," he said. "It's your friend, Tom."

"What?"

"Under the founding rules, if an athlete is deemed to associate with undesirable characters, he—"

I couldn't help myself. I stood up again. "Are you saying that Tom is undesirable? Like he's a criminal?"

"You must remember his prank with the net and the pigeons. And I heard about the toilet seat thing. And that's just this week. There've been fireworks, baking soda pranks and let's not forget that little incident with a gorilla suit."

"Let me get this straight," I said, reining in my anger. "I've been hanging out with this guy since kindergarten, and now, today, after playing on this team for more than three years, you decide that our friendship breaks the high school charter."

Coach Buckley dropped his papers. He stood and faced the wall away from me. Without looking at me, he spoke. "You can look at it that way if you want. But the final result is the same. You can no longer play on the team."

I had a lot of things I wanted to say to Coach Buckley. None of them would have helped the situation.

I kept my mouth shut. My brain kept working, though. My dad is in jail, I thought. My mom is in the hospital. I can no longer play the sport I love. My scholarship chances have just disappeared. And with the hospital bills mounting, there's no way to pay for college tuition.

Was there anything else?

Oh yeah. Death threats on the answering machine.

I almost wanted to laugh, it was so pitiful.

I stared at Coach Buckley's back. He was giving me such a lame excuse, I knew what this was really about. My dad. Principal Black had warned me about how people might react.

Maybe if I made a big stink about getting cut, someone would try to help. Like Principal Black or some of my teammates' parents.

After all, I was pretty good. People liked it when I helped the Titans win. But if I made a big stink, people would know I had been cut because of my dad.

Coach Buckley kept talking to the wall. "Believe me, Jack," he said. "I have no choice. You have to go."

He was right. I wasn't going to bring more shame on my dad by giving people another excuse to talk about him. So for me, there was no choice. I turned and walked out.

chapter thirteen

Everyone from the team had left the locker room by the time I got there. The room was empty except for Tom Sawyer.

"Hey," he said as I walked in. Big grin. Big freckles.

"Hey back," I said.

"I've been waiting for you. Good game," he said.

"Thanks," I said.

"Actually," he said, "great game. I mean you left a couple of guys hanging on to thin air. You went through them like a hot knife through butter. And that jumper at the end of the game. Man! Talk about a gut check."

"Thanks," I said. His excitement about the game only made things worse for me.

. He suddenly caught my mood and stopped talking.

I went and showered. When I got back, he was still waiting.

"I'm thinking," Tom said, "we should go do something fun. I mean, by now you must be feeling like those pigeons have zeroed in on you for target practice, again...and again...and again."

That brought a smile to my face. "Just because my mom's in the hospital and my dad's in jail?" I asked sarcastically.

I couldn't bring myself to tell him Coach had cut me from the team. That would have made it real. For now I wanted to pretend that Coach had not called me into his office.

"Yeah," he said, "something like that. And because your lower lip is dragging so bad you might trip over it."

He was trying to make me laugh again. I could tell by the tone of his voice. Instead I began to get mad. Not at him. At life. He had reminded me of how all the bad things were beginning to pile up.

"It's got a reason to drag," I said, feeling an unfamiliar sensation begin to fill my stomach. I work hard to not lose my temper, but I didn't feel like fighting it now. My words came out through clenched teeth. "I...don't...deserve... this..."

My anger swept over me like fire feeding on dead grass. I knew what was going to happen as I stepped toward a locker. But that didn't stop me. I loved every raging moment as I swung at the lockers. I brought my hand down from above my head as if I was swinging a hammer. Even in my anger, I wasn't dumb enough to punch out from my waist so that my knuckles hit first. I didn't want to hurt myself. I just wanted to pound out some of my anger.

So I hit the locker—hard.

I loved the impact of my fist against metal. I loved the loud bang. I loved the dent I made. And, briefly, I loved the pain that shot up my arm.

But only briefly.

I blinked back tears, shuddered at the pain and cradled my right hand with my left. My anger was gone, but it had probably left behind a broken knuckle. I could barely move the pinkie of my right hand.

"Ouch," I said in a small voice.

Tom stared at me with his eyes wide.

"It wasn't you," I told him quickly. My teeth were still clenched. Not from anger now, but from pain. "Just a bunch of things."

My hand really hurt. "And I thought life couldn't get any worse. But it has."

I tried to grin. "I don't think I can use this hand to shift. Can you take me to the hospital?"

chapter fourteen

The parking lot had long since emptied, which was good. My knuckle and pinkie finger were throbbing so badly I'm not sure I would have been able to talk to anyone about the game.

Tom's car was a bright blue Mustang, an older model he had bought cheap and fixed up himself. He loved that car and kept it shiny and clean, inside and out. So when we got in, I immediately noticed the small piece of yellow paper on the passenger side floor.

"Call the cops," I said, reaching for it with my left hand. "Someone littered in your car."

"Fell from the dash," Tom said, firing up the engine. "It's a notice to pick something up at the post office."

"What?" I asked.

"Dumb question," he answered. "How will I know what it is until I pick it up?"

"Maybe you ordered something," I said. "The question wasn't that dumb."

"Coming from a guy who's probably just busted his own hand, I think dumb is still the word that fits best."

He had a point.

I didn't say much as Tom drove us toward the hospital. Every bump in the road seemed to make the throbbing of my hand worse.

"I don't suppose," I finally asked without hope, "that you have any aspirin in the car?"

In his white lab coat, gray-haired Doc Tremblay was tall and thin. Doc had not only brought me into the world, but about twenty years before that, he had also delivered my father and mother. It wasn't something I was likely to forget; Doc reminded me every time I saw him.

I caught the faint smell of Old Spice aftershave as he leaned over me to inspect my hand.

"We'll wait for the X-ray results, of course," he said. "But either way, broken or not, we should splint it so you don't cause more damage. If it's not broken, we can take the splint off much earlier."

Doc straightened. He wore wire-rimmed glasses and his eyes pierced me like eagle's eyes as he asked his next question. "How did this happen, Jack? I don't recall seeing you get injured during the basketball game."

Doc, of course, had been at the game. Here in the emergency clinic, he'd been talking about the game almost nonstop as he looked at my hand.

"How did it happen?" I repeated.

"This have anything to do with your friend Tom?" Doc had known Tom a long time too.

And he'd seen Tom sitting with me in the waiting room.

"No," I said, "not really."

"Not really?"

"I lost my temper." There was no point in trying to hide it from Doc. "I punched a locker."

"Not too smart," he said, grinning. "But better a locker than a person."

"Like I'd do that," I said. "You know me better than that."

"You never know," Doc answered. "When your dad was your age, he had quite a temper."

"Right," I said. "And the sky is green."

"Ask him about it some time," Doc said as if Dad were waiting for me at home. "More than once I had to stitch him up after he got into a fight."

"Are you serious?" I said. "My dad? Mr. Accountant?"

"All I'm going to say is you should ask him about it some time. Young people tend to forget that their parents were once young too."

Doc's face softened. "This is all pretty rough on you, isn't it?"

"Mom in the hospital and Dad in jail, you mean?"

Doc nodded. "It's a safe guess that you lost your temper because you're under tremendous stress. It's not good for you to just pretend everything is all right. Long term, keeping things like that inside can literally kill a person—heart attacks, strokes. Healthy emotions help bodies stay healthy."

"Thanks," I said. "Now I can also worry about having a heart attack or a stroke."

He patted my shoulder. "Not for a while. Just take good care of yourself. With everything else your dad is facing, the last thing he needs to worry about is you."

I blinked a few times as Doc's words sank into my thick head: *With everything else your dad is facing, the last thing he needs to worry about is you.*

I'd been feeling so sorry for myself about how my world was falling apart that I'd forgotten how much worse it must be for him.

"You're right, Doc," I said slowly. "Things aren't going too well for him."

"He was almost crazy the day of your mom's accident," Doc said. "I think the worst of it was that he blamed himself."

"Himself?" I repeated, surprised.

"He kept saying he was supposed to be driving the car—over and over again. But your mom had volunteered to pick it up from the dealership at the last minute."

"Dealership?" I repeated.

"Where it was being serviced," Doc said. "Didn't your dad tell you any of this?"

I spoke without thinking. "Dad and I don't talk too much. Unless he's telling me how to better myself."

Doc sat down on a stool. "I'm a small-town doctor," he said. "And I know my patients too well to just worry about their medical health. So I hope you'll forgive me for offering some advice."

I nodded. My mind was still on one word: dealership.

"There's a lot about your dad you don't know," Doc said. "You're old enough now to start to think of him as a person. Not just as your father. I know it must be tough that he's always so strict with you. But if you find out where he's coming from, you'll be able to understand him. And anytime you understand a person, it's a lot easier to be friends."

Dealership.

"Anyway," Doc said, "enough lecturing. If your dad wants you to know about his past, that will be his decision, not mine."

I hardly heard Doc. But I kept hearing that one word echo through my head. Dealership.

Doc stood up. "Come on," he said. "I've got to splint that finger for you."

"Sure," I said.

I followed, or at least my body did. My mind was elsewhere the whole time Doc taped up my little finger.

Dealership.

chapter fifteen

I had a study break the next afternoon. I decided to use it to go see Mom at the hospital. I wasn't looking forward to it. Not after the phone call I had returned to Dad's lawyer at lunch.

I didn't much look forward to walking through the hospital either.

I'll bet any kid who had to write about a hospital visit would mention the smell first.

No matter how clean the wide and waxed hallway floors are, no matter how nicely painted the walls are, hospitals have that weird sweet smell of medicine and sickness and despair. At least that's the way it seemed to me as I followed a big male nurse down the hallway.

He was pushing an older woman in a wheelchair. She kept turning her little gray head on her thin neck to look at me. "I miss my children," she said again and again. "I miss my children."

She made me think of a tiny lost sparrow. She made me wonder how people could let their parents waste away in hospitals and nursing homes. She made me sad.

When I got to my mom's room, she was sleeping. The sadness inside me helped me to see her as a little girl lost in her dreams. I quietly pulled a chair up beside her bed and listened to her breathe.

The trouble was, most sleeping little girls don't have bruises and black eyes from a broken nose. And most sleeping little girls aren't held rigid by casts.

Moms have instinct, of course. Even in her sleep she knew I was close by. Her shoulders shifted a bit. She woke up and blinked her eyes.

"Sweet dreams?" I asked.

She smiled. She had shoulder-length dark hair. It was messed up from sleeping and made her look even younger than she already did. "It was more like being in the middle of a memory. A picnic. With you and your father."

Her smile dimmed as more memories returned. She was in a hospital, and my father was in jail.

I had something I didn't want to have to tell her.

With that instinct that moms have, she read it on my face.

"What is it, Jack?" she asked.

I held up my splinted finger. "Basketball injury," I said, giving her a big grin. I'd tell her about getting cut from the team later. A person shouldn't have to get more than one piece of bad news at a time. "Only a bad bruise, though. Not broken."

She knew me well enough to know my grin was fake.

"Uh-huh," she said. "So, what is it really?"

No sense in keeping the bad news from her.

"Dad decided not to pay the bail," I said. "He says he's going to stay in jail. He doesn't even want his lawyer anymore."

"What?"

"That's what I said," I told her. "His lawyer left a message at the school office for me this morning. When I called him at lunch, that's all he could tell me. He said he didn't know what Dad was doing. Dad wouldn't explain it to him."

"Your father's going to stay in jail," Mom said slowly.

I nodded.

Mom moved a hand out from under the bed covers and reached for mine. I took her hand and sat quietly.

There was nothing to say.

We sat like that for a long time. Then I had to head back to campus for classes.

After school I met Tom by my car in the lot behind the high school. It was a windy rainy day, with the kind of clouds that break apart long enough to tease you with a hope of sunshine, and then they mass together again to dump some more water.

The day matched my spirits.

Word had gotten around the school quickly that I had been cut from the team. Whenever people asked me about it, I just told them to talk to the coach. Which only made the rumors worse, I guess. Some people assumed I was cut because of my dad. Some assumed that Coach and I had a fight. Others assumed my injured hand made me quit. The only good news I could see was that no one had assumed it was because I wasn't good enough.

Not even Tom's usual big grin could lighten my mood.

"Where're we going?" he asked.

I didn't answer. I got into the car and reached over and unlocked his side.

He got in.

"Where're we going?" he repeated.

"Something weird is happening," I said.

"No kidding," he said. "I went to the post office at lunch to pick up that package and—"

"Dad won't talk to me about Mom's car accident," I said, interrupting Tom. I started the car and carefully looked back before easing out of the parking space. "I drove out to see him last night after my hand stopped throbbing, and he told me not to ask questions."

I stopped, put the car in first and drove forward. "It's like he doesn't care. He just wants to sit in jail and wait for his trial. Not only did he refuse to bail himself out, now he won't even talk to his lawyer."

The familiar houses and familiar trees and familiar stores flashed by as we cruised down the main road. And a thought I had been thinking again and again flashed through my mind. Could Dad really be guilty? I felt awful just wondering.

"But I'm not giving up," I said, shaking the thought away. "I'm not going to stop asking questions. If Dad won't answer them, maybe someone else will."

"Who?" Tom asked.

"Someone at the dealership," I said.

I slowed down for a curve. Turner Chev Olds was just ahead. I realized Tom had started to tell me something. "What did you say about the post office?" I asked.

"More weird stuff," Tom said. "I got a present, and it isn't even close to my birthday."

"You're right," I said. "That is weird."

"It gets weirder," Tom said. "The present was from your dad."

"What?" The only way Dad ever remembered my birthday was because Mom reminded him about it. Why would he...

"It gets even weirder," Tom said. "He gave me a cuckoo clock."

"A cuckoo clock?"

I slowed again to turn in to the dealership parking lot. A number of cars in the lot had balloons tied to their antennas. Everywhere big signs shouted in bright colors about rebates and low interest rates and low down payments. Behind the main sales floor was the service shop, a low gray building lined with big garage doors. That was our destination.

"Yeah," Tom said, "a cuckoo clock. Do you think he was trying to tell me something?"

I parked the car and we went inside the service shop. There was a front counter with a receptionist. Behind the front counter was a door that led to the work area. Customers were supposed to stay in this waiting area while the mechanics worked on their cars.

But I wasn't a customer. I had spent the last summer delivering car parts to outlying service stations, and I knew the receptionist.

"Hi, Belinda," I said. She was a middle-aged woman with a nice smile. "We're here to see Joe."

She waved us on back.

As we stepped through the door into the shop area, the blasts of the air guns that the mechanics used to tighten bolts got louder. Cars idled in different stalls as mechanics worked under their hoods; hoses were attached to the tailpipes to run the engine exhaust outside so no one would get carbon monoxide poisoning.

I looked around and saw Joe near the back, standing beside a truck, talking to a mechanic. Joe was the service foreman. His job was to make sure everything ran smoothly.

Joe saw me. I waved, and he waved back.

Tom and I waited for him to finish with the mechanic and walk toward us.

"You going to tell me what this is about?" Tom asked.

"I could," I said, "but I think you'll figure it out soon enough."

Joe was wearing dark blue coveralls. He was a short guy, probably around fifty years old, with a crew cut and close-cut sideburns that reached down his jawline. Joe walked in a bouncy way, almost like a monkey.

"Jack," he said as a greeting.

"Joe," I said, "you doing good?"

"Yeah," he said, "except for this stuff about your dad. Let me tell you, I don't believe none of it."

"Thanks," I said. "I don't believe it either. Can you help me check something?"

"What do you need?" Joe had to speak loudly above the clatter of the work going on around us.

"Well," I said, "I wondered if we could go through some old work orders."

Work orders were the written estimates and costs for repairs made on cars. They were carbon copied to be in triplicate. One for the records, one for the customer and one for the accounting department.

"I guess so," he said, leading us past motor parts on the way to his office. "You need something specific?"

I waited until he closed the door to his office. Sounds still reached us, but faintly.

"Well," I said, "I'd like to see the work order on my folks' car."

I gave him the date. It wasn't tough for me to remember. It was the date of Mom's accident.

He went to a filing cabinet, opened a drawer and shuffled through some papers.

Then he straightened and turned back toward us with a frown.

"Strange," he said. "There's no work order. You sure you gave me the right date?"

"Absolutely sure," I said.

He looked again.

"Strange," he repeated. "It's gone. What exactly were you looking for?"

Gone. That just proved to me there was something to look for. Otherwise the copy of the work order would be in Joe's files. Who took it? Trouble was, I didn't know exactly what I was looking for. I had just thought the paperwork would be a good place to start.

"What am I looking for?" I repeated slowly, thinking. Even if the work order had disappeared, I could at least talk to the mechanic. "Who worked on the car?"

Joe chuckled. "I can't remember what I had for lunch, much less who worked on what that far back. And without the work order..."

"Nuts," I said.

"Of course," Joe said, "the mechanics might remember. Your dad issues their paychecks. I'm sure they'd remember if they worked on his car. Give me a minute and I'll ask around."

Joe opened his door and wandered into the shop area.

Tom looked at me. "What are you looking for?"

"I kept this to myself because Ike asked me to. But Ike probably didn't know that the car had been in his shop on the day of Mom's accident. I'm just wondering if something happened to the car while it was here."

"What are you talking about?" Tom asked.

I told him about the brakes. How someone had adjusted them to work poorly. They hadn't been messed with enough to completely fail. But enough so that the car would not stop as quickly as normal.

"Wow," Tom said. "I don't get it. Why would someone want your mom to have an accident?"

"Not Mom," I said. "Dad. Dad was supposed to take the car home, but she came by to get it instead."

Tom thought for a moment. "But why would someone want to hurt your dad?"

"Maybe," I said, "because he knows a lot more about that missing money than he's told anyone?"

That was my hope. I'd thought about this for hours and hours, trying to come up with an answer. And that was the only one I could find.

Before Tom could say anything else, Joe opened the door and came into his office again.

He had a strange look on his small wrinkled face.

"Jack," he said, "I found out who worked on the car. But you can't talk to him. He's gone. Just like the work order."

"Gone?"

"Gone," Joe said. "As in quit. His name was Frank Gowan."

I remembered Frank from my summer here. He was a grimy guy with missing teeth and a handlebar mustache.

"Quit?" I felt like a brainless echo.

"He quit the day after he worked on your dad's car. Didn't even give a week's notice. He just called in at eight that morning and said he was leaving town."

"Weird," I said.

"That's not all," Joe said, shaking his head. "Frank was always borrowing money from someone. Always broke. When I asked where he wanted me to send his final paycheck, he told me he didn't need it."

Joe scratched his head. "For the life of me, I can't make any sense of it."

I could. If Frank had messed with the brakes, he wouldn't want to be found.

The bigger question was why he had messed with the brakes.

chapter sixteen

Several hours later, I was driving in the rain toward home. In those hours, Tom and I had stopped to visit Mom. She'd had a rough afternoon, and the doctor had given her a sedative. After we sat and watched her sleep for a while, I decided she wasn't going to wake up anytime soon. So I took Tom home and stayed for dinner when his mom invited me. When I arrived home I got a strange phone call. Someone with a mysterious whisper told me that if I wanted to know more about my dad, I should wait in the parking lot by the 7-Eleven. Then the caller hung up.

I drove to the 7-Eleven, scared and curious at the same time. I parked in front of the store window so nobody would try anything crazy on me. The rain began to pound on my windshield as I waited. And waited. After an hour, no one had shown up. So I gave up and headed home.

I had spent that whole hour thinking things through and wondering.

All I could figure was that if Frank Gowan had done something to my mom's brakes, he must have done it for someone who paid him a lot of money. Why else would he have left without his paycheck? And I bet that someone asked Frank to leave Turner so no one could ask him about the car later. My guess was that whoever had paid Frank was desperate.

But that only led to bigger questions. Who? Why?

I was convinced that this person had really been trying to do something to Dad, not Mom. But then I had to ask, why Dad? What had Dad done to make someone desperate enough to hurt him? And did it have anything to do with why Dad was in jail, refusing bail?

I decided it was too much of a coincidence to believe that these crazy things were not related.

Which only led to more questions. How were they related? What secrets was my dad keeping? And if he was innocent, why wasn't he acting like it? And who had called me to the 7-Eleven parking lot to let me sit, and why? No matter how much I strained my brain, I couldn't come up with any answers that made sense.

I turned in to my driveway and parked. The rain drummed steadily on the roof and hood. I dashed into the house to keep from getting too wet.

Inside I discovered why I had been sent to the parking lot. I also discovered I was not alone.

I heard a soft rustling—a whisper of danger that meant nothing until I felt something sharp in the middle of my back.

"Don't move," came a harsh whisper. "Don't try to turn around. I've got a gun."

Someone had come up behind me from the dark hallway that led to the bedrooms.

That same someone snapped off the light at the switch on the wall. That left us alone in the dark, me and someone with a gun and a harsh whisper.

"I won't move," I said as calmly as I could.

"Good." The whisper stayed harsh. "Now get on your knees. Then drop to your stomach and put your arms behind your back."

Slowly I did as I was told. Every second I expected the blast of pain that would follow a fired gun.

On my stomach with my hands behind my back, I heard more rustling. Then other, odd pulling sounds. It wasn't until I felt a thin cord around my wrists as the stranger tied my hands together that I figured it out. The person with the harsh whisper had tied me up with a lace from his shoe.

That meant this guy hadn't been expecting me. Otherwise he would have had something ready.

"Listen," the whisper said, placing a foot on my neck and pressing down hard.

As my face pressed deep into the carpet of our hallway, a dumb thought flashed through my head. I was glad I had vacuumed recently as part of my weekly chores. Were these the kinds of useless things that went through people's heads as they were about to die?

"Drop the questions," the whisper commanded. "Leave this thing alone, or your father will have a funeral to attend. Yours."

The foot pressed harder against my neck.

"Got it?"

"Ummmph," I said.

"Got it?" The foot eased off my neck.

"Got it," I said.

"Remember," the voice whispered, "we can find you anywhere. Anytime. You tell your dad, so he knows it too."

Without warning, the foot lifted off my neck. I heard a slight thud as something dropped onto the carpet beside me. And I heard a burst of footsteps as the stranger with the harsh whisper ran down the hallway.

Before I could even roll over, the front door opened and slammed shut, and he disappeared into the rain.

My heart was pounding so hard I wasn't sure if I could trust my ears. Was I really alone?

Finally I pushed myself to my knees.

The first thing I saw was a broom on the floor.

I'd been suckered. There had been no gun, only the end of a broom handle.

I needed to find some way to cut the shoelace and free my wrists. I walked into the kitchen, bending and twisting my neck to get some relief from the face mashing I had just endured.

With my elbow, I turned on the overhead light. That's when I saw that the kitchen had been trashed. Drawers had been pulled out. Cupboard doors stood open. Knives and forks lay all over the floor. Cereal boxes had been cut open, with cereal spilling in all directions.

And that wasn't the worst of it.

After cutting my wrists loose with a knife I found on the floor, I discovered the rest of the house was just as bad.

chapter seventeen

I called Sheriff Mackenzie first. Then Ike Bothwell.

Both got to the house at about the same time. Sheriff Mackenzie wore a rain slicker and carried a big flashlight. Ike showed up with water dripping from his cowboy hat.

I just told them someone had broken into the house. I didn't tell them about getting tied up by the man with the harsh whisper. Sheriff Mackenzie asked me and Ike to wait in the front hallway while he searched the house for clues. What surprised me as he walked away was that I did not hear big clunking footsteps. For a man so huge, he walked softly.

"What happened to your finger?" Ike asked me, pointing to the splint on my pinkie.

"Long story," I said. "Real long story."

Ike shook his head with sympathy. "You haven't had a very good run lately."

He didn't need to remind me. I'd been adding it up myself. Mom in the hospital, Dad in jail, me cut from the team, a badly bruised and splinted hand, an odd threat on the answering machine, not to mention a gun/broom handle in the back and a trashed house.

"Life's been better," I said. The only person I wanted feeling sorry for me was me.

I heard the back door open and close. I guessed it was Sheriff Mackenzie checking things out.

"Ike," I said, "when Doc splinted my finger, he told me a little about what Dad used to be like."

I'd hardly listened to Doc at the time because I'd been thinking about the car and how it had been at the dealership the day of the accident. But since then I'd been wondering about some of the other things Doc had said: *There's a lot about your dad you don't know...If you find out where he's coming from, you'll be able to understand him...*

"Doc told me Dad had a real temper when he was my age," I said. "That he got into fights and stuff. I can hardly believe that."

I thought about Doc's words: *Anytime you understand a person, it's a lot easier to be friends...If your dad wants you to know about his past, that will be his decision, not mine.*

"And Doc hinted about something Dad did. It kind of seemed like something bad that Dad's been hiding from me."

Ike kept his eyes on me for a long time before he spoke.

"Jack," Ike said, "my own father passed on about ten years ago. Let me just say I was happy we had become more than father and son. We were friends. Good friends. And after what I was like in my teens, I feel blessed that our relationship ended that way. When I was your age, I thought I knew everything. My father was just a stuffy rule-making drill sergeant. It was so bad, I nearly ran away from home and joined the navy."

"And?" I asked.

Ike shrugged. "One of those things that are way bigger than you realize at the time happened. I was wrapping up all these loose ends before I took off—you see, I had it planned. I had some books to return to the library, and the librarian said something in passing about my dad. I discovered she had been his girlfriend back when they were in high school. I was surprised to think about my dad in that way—that he'd once been a kid like me who worried about girls and pimples and doing stupid things. It got me to thinking about him as a person. Which got me to trying to think of things from his point of view. You know, how he saw me as a son, instead of just how I saw him as a father. It helped."

Ike shrugged again. "It wasn't like we instantly became friends, but I stopped making it so hard for us, and soon enough, we discovered how important we were to each other."

I nodded. "But what did Dad do when he was my age? I mean, what was Doc talking about?"

"Did you hear a single word I said?" Ike asked. "Or were you worrying so much about yourself that my story about the high school librarian didn't sink in?"

I looked at the floor. I guess I wanted the big story, not the little story.

"Jack," Ike said, "it's not important what your dad did or did not do. It's important that you think of him as more than a rule-making father."

Ike grinned, catching how serious he'd gotten. "'Course, I don't blame you for being curious. But if your dad hasn't told you, I'm not going to. You'll have to ask him."

Before I could say anything else, Sheriff Mackenzie returned.

"All I found," he said, "was a trampled flower bed beneath a window, like somebody was looking inside to make sure the house was empty. But with this rain, it's just mud. The footprints are useless."

The big man scratched his head. "So at this point," he said, "all I can tell you is the obvious. Whoever was here was looking for something. Any idea what?"

"None," I said.

"Did you see anyone?" the sheriff asked.

I thought about the whispered threat to make things worse for my dad if I told anyone about the intruder. But I didn't want to lie either.

"Whatever I tell you," I said, " we need to keep secret."

I explained why. Then I explained what had happened, even about the phone call that sent me to the 7-Eleven. Then I pulled the two pieces of muddy shoelace from my back pocket. The shoelace I'd cut off my wrists.

Sheriff Mackenzie talked as he walked to the front door. "Obviously someone wanted you out of the house, Jack. When you drove up in the rainstorm, he couldn't hear the car. You're lucky you didn't get hurt. Sometimes people who walk in on robberies do. But the fact that he had to use a broom handle showed he wasn't armed.

"This could have been someone simply looking for valuables, except for two things. Most people don't look for valuables in the kitchen by ripping apart cereal boxes. From the mess he made, I'd bet this guy was angry he couldn't find what he wanted."

Sheriff Mackenzie shone his flashlight at the lock on the door and at the doorframe itself. "And the second thing is this: no scratches or anything like that around the lock, or on the back door. And all the windows were latched on the inside. What this tells me is that someone got in here using a key, or he is an extremely professional burglar. And we don't have those in Turner. So it must have been someone who has access to the house or someone sent in from out of town. Either possibility raises big questions."

The phone rang, interrupting Sheriff Mackenzie.

I answered within three rings. It was Judy Bothwell, Ike's wife.

"I need to speak to Ike," she said. Her voice sounded higher pitched than usual. Like she was scared.

I carried the cordless phone back to where the men stood and handed the phone to Ike.

He listened carefully, and then he said good bye. He handed the phone back to me.

"Sheriff," Ike said, "looks like you have more business tonight. That was Judy. She just got a call from the security guy who stops by the dealership several times every night."

"Yes?" Sheriff Mackenzie asked.

"Looks like someone tore a few things apart inside the dealership."

"Does he think you were robbed?" Sheriff Mackenzie asked.

"No," Ike said, "mainly it looks like someone tore apart Jack Senior's office."

Jack Senior. Dad.

Ike pressed his lips together grimly. "My guess is that someone was looking for the same thing he couldn't find here."

chapter eighteen

I didn't want to go to the basketball game on Friday night. And I did want to go. In the end, I decided to listen to it on the radio—I decided I didn't want people pointing me out as the kid whose Dad was in jail or wondering why I wasn't playing.

I listened to it in the spare bedroom at Tom's house. I was staying there because Sheriff Mackenzie had suggested it would be safer than staying home alone.

So I sat in the corner of a room on the upper floor of a house down the street from my own. I felt very alone. Just me and the tinny voice from the cheap radio on the shelf over a narrow single bed.

"Well, folks," the announcer was saying, "the Titans are going into tonight's game without the help of one of their key players, Jack Spencer. Rumors fill the stands as to exactly why he's off the team. I mean, Spencer was the one player who could turn a game around, and tonight the Titans are going to really miss him. Lots of folks are wondering why the coach let this kid go."

In the background, I heard the usual crowd noises. The noises that would swallow me up and get my blood going if I were on the gym floor, throwing baskets to warm up before the game.

"For those of you who have been on the planet Mars," the announcer said, "this has not been a good month for Jack Spencer. It started with a car accident that put his mother in the hospital, followed by the total shock to the community when his father was arrested and charged with embezzlement; this young man has faced some difficult times. When we asked Coach Buckley why Spencer was dropped from the team, Buckley's only comment was that it was an internal matter. Whatever that means. But it has led some folks to wonder—"

I snapped the radio off. I already knew what some folks were wondering. Whether I had anything to do with my dad's alleged illegal activities. Whether, somehow, I had helped him during my summer job at the dealership.

I sat on the edge of the bed and buried my face in my hands.

This was so unfair. I didn't deserve to be sitting here, in someone else's home without my family.

My mom was a good person. My dad was a good person. I wasn't bad. We went to church. We helped charities. Shouldn't this bad stuff happen to people who lied and cheated and tried to hurt other people?

I mean, why would a good God allow bad things to happen to good people? We were on his side, not against him.

I started to get that feeling that had made me pound a locker.

I was getting mad.

I backed up and thought for a second. And I realized I was mad at God. I mean, people wonder about him all the time, whether he really exists and what that means. Well, I was almost ready to decide he wasn't out there. Or if he was, he really wasn't paying attention. And if he wasn't paying attention to me, why should I pay attention to him?

I sat there on the edge of the bed, getting madder and madder.

Then I started to think about my dad. You can only see God if you look for him in the things he has made. Kind of like you can see artists in their paintings.

My dad, though, I saw every day.

And he didn't seem to be paying much attention to me either. At least not the kind of attention I wanted. Had he taken the effort to get me a gift for no apparent reason like he had for Tom? Had he ever just patted me on the back? Had he ever told me I was good at something? No. He just told me how to be better. Dad's job was to be the policeman of my life. And there he was, in jail himself.

These thoughts got me pretty worked up. I began to pace back and forth in the small room.

I felt like a caged animal, ready to explode.

I put on my shoes and went into Tom's bedroom and grabbed his basketball.

In the driveway, I shot basket after basket, trying to get rid of my anger. It helped that I had to concentrate harder to shoot with my off hand, thanks to my splint.

But the anger stayed with me.

After an hour of shooting baskets, I started to feel pretty good about how many shots went in, even without my best shooting hand. Then I decided to head back up to the spare bedroom. I wanted to be in bed before Tom and his parents got back from the basketball game, so I wouldn't have to talk about it.

The anger stayed with me in the dark as I stretched out on the narrow bed.

It stayed with me as I fell asleep, tossing and turning. It probably stayed with me as I slept, because I had horrible dreams about a giant cuckoo clock. The wooden bird inside kept jumping out and laughing at me. I threw a basketball at it, but the bird just jumped back inside the clock, and the basketball bounced harmlessly away.

Then, in my dream, the cuckoo bird got loose and started to fly. It chased me around and around a tiny jail cell, flapping at my head.

I woke up with a start.

And I realized the cuckoo bird in my dream had been trying to tell me something.

chapter nineteen

I knocked quietly on Tom's bedroom door.

No answer.

I knocked a little louder but not too loud.
I didn't want to wake up his parents.

I heard a groan from his room.

I pushed the door open.

"Tommy-wommy," I whispered, "wakey,
wakey. Time for bottle and burp."

"Mom?" Tom croaked, still half asleep.

"No," I said. I snapped on the light. "Forget the bottle and burp. I need to see something."

Tom's bed was against the far wall beside a life-size Michael Jordan poster. His floor was littered with clothes. I looked at Tom. His hair twisted in all directions. There was a red line on his cheek, where his face had pressed into his pillow, and drool on the side of his chin. At the other end of the bed, his feet stuck out from under the blankets.

I crossed the bedroom, stepping carefully to avoid Tom's dirty socks.

His eyes finally opened and focused as I stood staring at him.

"Ack!" he said. "I'm having a nightmare!"

"Where's your cuckoo clock?" I said.

He rubbed his eyes. He squinted at me. He squinted at his alarm clock. He squinted back at me.

"Quarter to five in the morning and you want to see a cuckoo clock?"

"Yes," I said.

"Paint a bunch of numbers on your face and look in the mirror," he said. He pulled the blankets over his head. "Then you'll see a cuckoo that looks like a clock. Go away."

"I'm serious," I said. "Where is it?"

"I can't hear you," he said, jamming his pillow over his head. "I can't hear you."

I pulled his closet door open. More clothes spilled out. I grabbed a tennis racket from the top shelf to poke around in the clothes.

"What's this?" I said. "A big stuffed Barney doll?"

"Yeah, right," Tom said. "Nice try."

"Help me, Tom," I said. "Or I'll tell everyone at school I found a big Barney doll in your closet. And I'll tell them it was wearing Batman underwear."

He groaned again. "That's low. Real low."

"Only because I'm desperate," I said. "Where is it?"

"Under my bed," he answered.

"Under your bed?"

He was sitting up now, wearing a Mickey Mouse T-shirt that I decided to remain silent about.

"Under my bed. I was saving it to give to my mom on her next birthday."

He caught my frown. "Give me a break," he said. "What am I going to do with a cuckoo clock? Besides, your dad never comes over here—he'll never see where it is. It's not like he and I are friends or anything."

"Exactly," I said. I was already on my knees, fishing under the bed with my left hand. I was afraid of what I might touch. "Which is why I want to look at the clock."

My hand bumped against a box. I pulled it out. I opened it and lifted out the cuckoo clock. It was about the size of a toaster.

"What do you mean, 'exactly'?" Tom asked.

"He had to have some reason for sending it to you," I said. "But not because you're friends. So, what? It's just too strange."

I held the clock above my head and looked at its bottom. Four screws—one in each corner—held the bottom in place.

I glanced over at Tom and his twisted red-brown hair. "Well," I said, "maybe the cuckoo part isn't so strange."

"Ha, ha," Tom said.

I ignored him as I looked through the mess on top of his dresser. I found what I needed: a penknife. I began to unscrew the bottom of the clock.

"Hey! What are you doing?" he asked. "That's a perfectly good clock. And my mother's birthday is less than two weeks away..."

"Someone is looking for something Dad had," I said, working on the next screw.

"Like what?"

"Like something they didn't find at our house or in his office. And maybe he knew someone would come looking for whatever it is."

The screws were tiny. I started on the third one.

"And you're thinking it's in the clock?" Tom asked.

I unscrewed the fourth screw. The bottom of the clock fell into my hand. Along with a computer disk.

"I'm not thinking it," I said. I grinned as I held up the disk. "I know it."

chapter twenty

Ike Bothwell drove a gleaming black Blazer 4x4—I was his passenger in it Saturday at noon as we went to visit his brother, Ted, outside of Turner.

It was a great day, at least in terms of weather. Windless and cloudless, the Indiana sky stretched deep blue above the distant fields. With the sunroof open, I could see straight up. Air flowed over us in a rush of sound and sensation.

In terms of anything else, I was less sure how great the day was.

It might have been the same for Ike. He seemed impatient and had a hard time keeping the Blazer at the speed limit. The trees and fenceposts that lined either side of the road were as much of a blur as the morning had been.

At 5:00 AM, after finding the computer disk in the cuckoo clock, Tom and I had plugged it into his computer. We soon discovered that Tom didn't have the application to open the disk.

Tom managed to go back to sleep. Not me. I did a lot of pacing back and forth until 8:00 AM when I decided it was finally late enough to call Ike Bothwell. The dealership, I guessed, had the computer program that would read Dad's disk, and I wanted Ike to help me.

Ike was interested but couldn't meet me until about 11:00, so I had to pace back and forth a bunch more. I couldn't wait to find out what was on the disk. What mattered so much to Dad that he had to hide it in a cuckoo clock?

During that pacing, I asked myself again and again if I should just drive up to South Bend and ask Dad. But I told myself again and again that if he hadn't said anything to me about it earlier, there must be some reason for his secrecy.

Finally, Ike picked me up in his Blazer and we drove to the dealership.

When we plugged in the computer disk, we found good news and bad news. The good news was that we could read the disk. The bad news was that it was a complicated spreadsheet—hundreds of numbers in dozens of columns—that just raised more questions.

There was, however, one person who could read those numbers and make sense of them, Ike told me grimly. And that's where we were headed.

Suddenly, Ike turned onto a long driveway. The house at the end looked like a southern mansion, with big columns on each side of the door. It gleamed white and clean in the sun; from a distance it looked like a beautiful diamond set in the emerald green of the perfect lawn that surrounded it.

Ike parked beside the garage. He hopped out without taking the time to close the sunroof. With the sky so blue, there was zero chance of rain.

I followed Ike up to his brother's house. We stood in the shade of the wide porch next to the gleaming columns as we waited for someone to answer the doorbell.

Ted did not make us wait long.

He seemed surprised to see us but covered it quickly. "Come on in," he said, opening the door wide. Ted was in his sixties and had been divorced for years. He was taller and slimmer than his brother Ike. Instead of Ike's choice of checkered shirts and jeans, Ted usually dressed as if he'd just stepped out of a men's fashion magazine. Even on a Saturday at home, he wore navy slacks and a silk shirt. "It's good to have company," he added as we walked through the door.

In the wide hallway, our footsteps echoed loudly.

Ted ushered us to a sitting area. The chairs

were expensive leather, and the bronze statues made equally expensive-looking decorations.

"What can I do for you?" Ted asked. "I mean, Ike, you hardly ever drop by. And Jack, I don't think you've been here before, have you? I don't expect you two just happened to be in the area."

Ted's smile didn't seem real. His teeth were Hollywood white, and his face was so smooth and tight it looked almost shiny. I knew he'd had a lot of work done on his teeth, and people said plastic surgery kept the wrinkles away. And his hair was unnaturally dark—probably dyed.

"Well, Ted," Ike began, "how about we go into your office. I've got something on a computer disk I'd like you to see. Maybe you can help us make some sense of it."

Ted shrugged. His million-dollar smile looked forced but never left his face.

"Sure, brother," he said, "I'll do my best."

Ted Bothwell's second-story office showed the same expensive taste as the rest of the house. His desk and the bookshelves were made of deep, rich walnut wood. More bronze statues were artfully scattered around the room. Oil paintings filled the walls. A large picture window opened onto the landscaped gardens below.

Ted flicked on his computer.

Ike handed him the disk.

"What do we have here?" Ted asked as he inserted the disk into the computer.

"I'm not sure," Ike said, choosing his words carefully. "It's accounting stuff. Which, as you know, is just a jumble of numbers to me."

Ted nodded. Ike ran the sales side of the dealership, but Ted was the businessperson who held it together.

The hard drive whirred. Ted leaned over his desk and made some quick movements with the computer's mouse.

"You're right," Ted said a few seconds later. "This is an accounting spreadsheet. Looks like it's information from the dealership."

"That was as near as I could tell," Ike said. "The only thing I could see for sure was the date it was last adjusted." The computer had recorded the date the files were last opened.

"Looks like these numbers were last touched about five weeks ago," Ike continued. "If I had to guess, I'd say that disk holds a backup of all the accounting files for the dealership."

Ted clicked the mouse back and forth without saying anything. After another minute, he nodded. "I'd say you're right."

"Excuse me," I said. "Do you mind if I get a glass of water?"

Ted spoke without taking his eyes off the computer screen. "Sure, downstairs in the kitchen."

I left them in Ted's office.

I headed to the kitchen for water. But I hurried. I wanted to give myself some time to look around.

On my way to the kitchen, I passed a bedroom. Silently, I slipped inside to check out the closet, guessing there would be shoes in there.

What I saw first was a pair of Nikes. I had hoped I might find one shoe without a lace, and the other with a match to the pieces Sheriff Mackenzie had taken from my home as evidence the night someone had broken in. But both shoes were laced. And both shoelaces were new and clean.

The Nikes, though, were caked with dried mud.

I picked up the shoes and walked back toward the office.

chapter twenty-one

When I entered the office, Ted was still at his desk facing the computer. Ike was in a chair across from the desk.

Without saying a word, I gave the mud-caked shoes to Ike.

Ike set them in his lap.

I quietly sat in another chair. I was sad for Ike.

Ike studied the shoes for a long time while his brother watched him.

I could see from Ted's face that he knew what Ike knew. But Ted didn't say a thing. Neither did I. We both waited for Ike.

"Quite the rainstorm we had the other evening," Ike finally said. "Don't suppose that was when these shoes got muddy?"

"I go running every evening," Ted answered.

"Funny," Ike said. "These laces are new. No mud. Like maybe you replaced them since the rainstorm."

"Laces break," Ted said.

Ike sighed. "I wish I could believe you, but I'm up against a few things that say otherwise."

The room got so quiet that the whir of the computer's hard drive sounded like a jet on a runway.

"See," Ike said, "Sheriff Mackenzie's got a couple of pieces of a muddy shoelace that were probably once in a shoe just like one of these. I'm guessing that these days the police can match the mud from the shoelace to mud from a flower bed at the Spencer house."

"What are you trying to say?" Ted asked. But Ted knew. I could tell by the rigid way he held his shoulders and neck.

"Someone broke into the Spencer house. Someone who had a key to get in. Someone who, say, could have easily borrowed Jack senior's keys down at the dealership when his car was being serviced. Someone who could quickly run out to make a spare set and return the keys within the hour. That same someone tied Jack Junior up with a muddy shoelace that could have come from one of these shoes."

"The same someone," I added, "who could pay Frank Gowan to rig the brakes on my parents' car—and the same someone who could destroy a work order without getting caught."

Ted stood, bracing himself by placing his hands palms down on his desk. "Are you accusing me?!"

"Sit down," Ike said in a tired voice. "I've known you all my life. I can tell when you're pretending to be angry."

After a moment, Ted sat.

"When Jack brought me this disk this morning," Ike said, still in a tired voice, "it didn't take me long to see what it meant. It's our dealership's accounting information.

Within twenty minutes I was able to figure out why the dealership has been losing so much money."

I'd sat with Ike as he went over the figures. Fake loans had been set up for people who had never bought cars from the dealership. Cars and trucks that didn't exist were listed as inventory. Payroll payments had been made to employees who weren't employees. And it looked like it had been happening for years and years and years—a couple of thousand dollars lost in one spot, a couple of thousand in another. Until it added up to close to half a million dollars.

"The man who did it is in jail," Ted said. "Jack Senior."

"Trouble is," Ike answered, "there was something else on this disk. Bank account numbers. Accounts that belong to you."

Silence.

"So I knew I needed to make this visit," Ike said. "And I asked Jack to look around for a pair of shoes with a missing shoelace. Because I still couldn't believe my own brother could do this to me."

"Believe it then," Ted said. He opened his desk drawer. He pulled out a pistol and pointed it at Ike's chest. "And if you still can't believe it, here's more proof."

chapter twenty-two

"Why?" Ike asked. His voice didn't sound like the voice of a man facing a pistol. "Why steal from me? If you didn't think you were getting paid enough, all you had to do was ask."

"Why?" Ted said. "I'll tell you why."

Ted's eyes narrowed and his cheeks tightened. He looked like a mean dog.

"It's your dealership," Ted said. "Even though I'm your brother, I'm just a paid employee. I've watched you take the profits for years."

"Your bonus every Christmas has matched what I took in profit," Ike said. "And I was the one who risked the money to start the dealership in the first place."

"You're married to a beautiful woman who loves you," Ted continued, not showing any sign he had heard Ike. "My wife left me years ago. Left me so alone."

"Your wife left you because of the way you treated her. She begged you to go to counseling with her to help your marriage work out."

"You have everything I don't," Ted continued in his mean, hateful voice. "Your life is so much better than mine. And I despise you for it."

"I have diabetes, I weigh too much and I've lost my hair," Ike said, still in a calm steady voice. "Your house is bigger than mine. You have everything you need. All the bad things in your life have happened by your choice. How can you be jealous? How can you say my life is better than yours?"

"Because you don't fall asleep every night thinking about an old couple who nearly died in a car accident that was really your fault."

"What?" Ike said.

"Who do you think was driving—drunk— that night?" Ted said. "And how many lives did I mess up because of it?"

This was making zero, zero sense to me. Ike, too, sat with his mouth open in surprise.

"It wasn't Jack?" Ike asked.

Jack? My dad? Some other Jack? What were they talking about?

"You figure it out," Ted said. "I'm tired of this conversation."

He got up and walked around the desk, keeping the pistol pointed at Ike's chest. I wondered if I should make a dive for the pistol. But I only wondered for a second. Fingers can pull triggers faster than bodies can leap across rooms.

"Are you going to kill me?" Ike asked without fear.

"No. Murder would be stupid when all I have to do is get on an airplane and leave the country. I've got your money. Without it, the dealership is in big enough trouble. I've taken enough from you."

"I see," Ike said calmly.

Suddenly Ted screamed. "See! See! This is exactly what I'm talking about. You're about to lose everything you have, and you just sit there with a smile. Life is horrible! Figure it out! Suffer like I do!"

Just as suddenly as Ted started screaming, he stopped.

"No," he said, "I'm not going to kill you. But it might be a while until someone finds you."

chapter twenty-three

After taking Ike's keys from him, Ted pushed us into his storage shed. It was built of brick, and he locked it on the outside with a padlock. The only window in it was on the back wall, about as high as I could reach. But reaching it wouldn't help. It was a small window. Maybe a basketball could get through, but that would be about it. I certainly couldn't. And Ike and his big belly certainly couldn't either.

Shortly after Ted slammed the door shut on us, we heard him start Ike's Blazer. We heard the motor purr as he drove it around behind the shed. He parked it on a wide round patio made of flat stones set into the ground. Then we heard silence as he shut it off, followed by the click of the truck door and a slam as he shut it again.

"He's hiding the truck from the road and driveway," Ike said. "No one will guess we're here."

I nodded glumly. "And it's not like this is a luxury hotel."

It wasn't. The most I could do was step once or twice in any direction. There was a lawn mower in the corner, and rakes and other garden tools hung on one wall. Another wall had sports gear on shelves— an old tennis racquet, a can of tennis balls, a baseball glove. It was hot in the shed, with a horrible smell of rotting grass from the underside of the lawn mower.

"Could be worse," Ike said. "We could be stuck in the trunk of a car, or be dead."

"Yeah," I said. "It could be worse."

I turned to the door and banged my shoulder against it. It didn't budge. When

I turned back, Ike was moving boxes and gardening equipment.

"Might as well make ourselves comfortable," he said. He grinned. "In fact, it might be a nice break to stay away from the dealership on a Saturday."

"Ike," I said, "your brother is driving to the airport so he can disappear with your money."

"Not good," Ike said.

"So how can you just sit there so calmly?" I said. "I'd be going nuts."

"Would it do any good? Would it bring Ted or the money back?"

"No, but—"

"Jack," Ike said, "here's the deal about life. It's difficult. You're always going to have problems to solve. And most important, God doesn't owe you anything. Once you realize that, and once you decide to always do the best you can with what you have, life isn't that tough anymore."

In the shaft of sunlight that came through the high small window, Ike must have seen that I didn't quite understand.

He smiled. "If you're expecting it to be hot in the middle of an Indiana winter, you'll be disappointed. Right? But if you dress in warm clothes because you know there's snow on the ground, the cold won't bother you. You know you just have to get through the winter."

I thought about that and nodded slowly.

"Think of life here on earth as a training camp for your soul," Ike said. "The way God designed it, all the troubles and temptations we face are things to help us learn and grow. He's helping us get ready for the journey our souls take after we die. If you're here on earth expecting life to pamper you, you'll always be disappointed."

Ike's voice became softer. "And after enough disappointment, you'll become old and bitter like my brother."

"I think I get it," I said. And I did. I felt my own anger at God sliding away. "Dad's in jail, Mom's in the hospital, and I can't play basketball. None of that's too exciting. But there are lots of people who have it worse. And maybe a year from now..."

"Do the best you can with what you have," Ike said.

"Yeah," I said. I looked for a place to sit. I had to move a can of gasoline so I could lean my back against the wall. I shook the can but heard nothing.

"Too bad this is empty," I said, joking. "Otherwise we could use it to start a fire and send up a smoke signal. That would bring someone to find us."

Ike gave me a strange look——as if I had just given him a great idea. He pulled his cigar lighter out of his pocket.

"Come on," I said. "Like we're going to burn up the shed with us inside? Just so the fire department can find our bodies?"

Ike stood up. He dusted the seat of his pants with his hands. Then he pushed a box beneath the window.

"Stand on this," he said. "Tell me what you see outside."

I stood on it and pushed up on my tiptoes, leaning against the wall to keep my balance. I could just see over the windowsill.

"Nothing," I said.

"Nothing? No garbage can filled with junk we could burn?"

"Nothing," I said, "except for your Blazer."

"Ouch," Ike said.

"Ouch?"

"It would send up a good smoke signal."

"You're not serious!" I said.

"What's the choice? Sit and wait while Ted gets away? It might take a couple of days for someone to find us." Ike grinned. "Besides, if I can get that half a million back, it's worth a lot more than a truck..."

I looked at the shiny black Blazer. The beautiful, shiny black Blazer.

"Ouch," I said. I climbed off the box.

"Now that I think about it," he continued, "Ted did park it on that stone patio, so we wouldn't have to worry about a fire spreading."

Ike was right. Much as it hurt my insides to think of that beautiful truck sending up our smoke signal, it was better than letting Ted get away.

But another thought hit me as I stared at the truck. "There's one tiny problem, Ike.

We're in here. The truck is way out there. How do we start the fire?"

Ike frowned. "Good point," he said. Then he sighed and settled back. "I guess it will be a long wait. Worst thing is, I drank too much coffee this morning. Already I have to..."

That was not a pleasant thought. The shed was too small and hot. And the smell of rotting grass was bad enough.

Looking around the shed for ideas, I spotted something on the shelf behind Ike. Something round. I stepped past Ike and pulled the basketball down. I tossed it into the air as I thought. Then I started spinning it on my forefinger. I spun it like a globe as I said, "If you're really willing to burn that truck, I think I've got an idea."

I stopped the grimy old basketball.

"All it's going to take," I said, "is the free throw of my life."

chapter twenty-four

If the morning had seemed like a blur, Saturday afternoon ran in double fast-forward.

Less than three hours later, I was at the jail. I squirmed on an unpadded metal chair in the waiting area. By now I knew the routine. Sit and twiddle my thumbs while a guard went to get Dad. Then sit and talk about nothing for the twenty minutes they allowed us together. And drive home depressed.

But that was the old jail routine.

Today was going to be different.

Yes, I had to sit and wait like before. Yes, I only had twenty minutes to spend with Dad. But today we weren't going to talk about nothing. And I wasn't going home depressed.

When the guard ushered Dad into the small visiting room, I tried to look at my dad as if he were someone else. Someone who had once been my age and had once had the same fears and worries and hopes. I tried to look at Dad as if he were the scared kid that Ike had told me about on the night of a car accident, more than twenty years ago. Looking at Dad in that way helped. It was as if I suddenly saw him as a real person instead of a remote kind of king who sat in judgment of everything I did.

I needed to see him that way to say what I wanted to say.

"Hello, Jack." Dad lowered himself into his chair as if he were an old man.

"Hi, Dad."

"How is your mother?"

"She's fine. Actually she's more than fine. The doctors are taking her off the painkillers." And, I thought, she knows about Ted and who really stole the money.

"Good. You have a safe drive here?"

"Yes, sir. No speeding tickets."

"Good."

I waited for him to say something else. Anything else. Anything more than questions about the weather. He didn't.

"Dad..." I filled my lungs with air as if I were about to dive into deep dark water. Which I guess I was. I let the air out. "I know about the accident."

"Mom's accident?"

"No, yours. The one that hurt those two old people."

There. I had said it. Now would he really talk to me about it?

Dad froze. "Who told you?"

"Ike," I said. "This morning. I made him tell me."

While we were waiting for the fire department to show up, I had convinced Ike to explain what Ted meant about the accident.

Now it was Dad's turn to let out a long breath.

"Dad," I said. This was way worse than the birds and the bees talk he had once given me. "Is that why you're always so hard on me? Because you're afraid if you give me any freedom, I might do the same kind of thing? I mean, Ike and Doc both told me you used to be pretty wild."

Dad thought for a moment before answering. I didn't push him.

"When I was your age I thought I knew everything." He spoke with his eyes closed. "I didn't listen to my parents or to the people in my church. I did stupid things. And one of those stupid things was to drink alcohol. When I had too much to drink, I got into fights."

He kept his eyes closed. "The night of the accident, I'd had so much to drink that I can't even remember getting into the car. When I woke up the next morning, I was in the hospital. The police told me that I had driven through a stop sign. The car that I hit..."

He stopped because his voice was so shaky. A few seconds later he started again.

"It was an old couple. Tourists from out of state. They were really hurt bad. I tried to visit them at the hospital. Their son and two daughters had flown in to be with them. And their grandchildren. There was nothing I could do to take back what I had done. The family wouldn't even talk to me. You cannot imagine the nightmares and regrets. All because of one stupid thing I had done."

This was my dad. A real person. I wanted to cry, thinking about the pain he hid from the world.

He opened his eyes again. "In answer to your question: Yes. Watching you grow up, I saw that you could be just like me. At least, like me before the accident. I thought the best thing I could do was to be so strict that you'd never get loose and wild and do something that would take the joy out of the rest of your life."

If I didn't say it now, I would never say it.

"That's not fair, Dad. You can't make me into a robot. I mean, even God lets us make choices."

For a second, I thought he would get cold and distant, the way he always did when I tried to argue with him. Instead he said, "You're right. I'm just beginning to see how bad things can turn out when you try to control everything."

Wow. Dad had just admitted he was wrong about something.

"Controlling things like the fraud and embezzlement charges?"

This time he did become cold and distant.

"I want to know why you decided to plead guilty to those charges," I said.

He stared at me for a long time. I wondered if he was deciding to tell me I had no right to speak to him that way.

But he didn't get mad at me. When he finally spoke, it was in such a quiet voice that I could hardly hear him.

"Look," he said, "I am guilty. I did steal from my best friend. Now maybe you should go."

It nearly broke my heart. Now that I could see him as more than just my father, I realized how proud a man he was. I realized how much it would cost him to have the world think he was a thief. And how much of a sacrifice he was making for my sake.

The words came out of my mouth before I realized I was saying them out loud.

"I love you," I said. "We never talk about our feelings, but I want you to know I love you."

His lean face softened, and his eyes went from the dull stone of bleakness and hopelessness to something warmer, something filled with light.

"And there's something else," I said. "The man who really stole from Ike Bothwell has been arrested. And I know why you decided to take the blame."

"What!"

"They let me be the one to give you the news. When I leave, you can come home with me. You're free."

I told him all that had happened. How the fire department had rescued us from the storage shed because of the huge smoky fire from the burning Blazer. How the police had found Ted Bothwell at the airport, about to disappear with his brother's money.

And Dad told me his side of the story. Six weeks earlier he had discovered a tiny accounting mistake. As he tried to unravel it, he discovered more and more mistakes. It was like tugging at one loose end and untangling a whole ball of string. At the other end, he had found Ted Bothwell.

But that had put him in a bad position. How could he break Ike's heart by telling him his own brother had been stealing from him? So Dad had gone to Ted and promised him he would keep the secret if Ted returned all the money in two weeks.

But Ted had used those two weeks to change the computer files, to make them point to Dad as the thief. Then Ted had arranged to have Dad's brakes messed up. Ted had wanted Dad out of the way, so Dad wouldn't be able to fight for his own innocence.

Mom had been hurt instead, and Ted had gone to the police with his new computer files. He decided to go after Dad legally, before Dad could show the police the original accounting files.

After that, Ted had told Dad how much worse it could get for me and Mom while he was in jail. How he could arrange for me to get cut from the basketball team. How easy it would be to hurt me. How easily he could smother Mom with a pillow.

He had forced Dad to make the only real choice: Take the blame and stay in jail to protect us. Even though Dad had a set of computer files to clear himself, he wasn't sure it was enough proof by itself. After I got cut from the team, he realized Ted might carry through on his other threats. He couldn't risk our getting hurt.

After Dad explained this to me, I had a little news of my own. The news I had been hanging on to because it was the best of all.

"Dad," I said, "a person has to wonder how Ted could have gotten this way. Why he was so bitter and unhappy that he could hate his own brother for being happy in life."

"True," Dad said. "After he'd taken the money and it looked like he might get caught, I can understand why he got desperate enough to try to kill someone to protect himself. But it looked like he had everything, so why would he steal in the first place? And from his brother..."

"I've learned something," I said. "From you and from Ike. Sometimes life isn't fair, but you just do the best you can."

"What does that have to do with Ted?" Dad asked.

"Your car accident all those years ago," I said. "You took the blame and moved on and did the best you could, right?"

"When the police investigated, I didn't deny I was driving," he said. "I lost my license for a couple of years and was sentenced to community work, which was a huge break from the judge. It was a lot better than having a criminal record. I decided after a break like that, I had to change. So, yes, I did the best I could."

I was proud of Dad. He could have become bitter and hated himself and everyone. Instead he tried to make up for that one big mistake, even if it meant being too strict on me. I respected him for the choice he made.

"Ted, though," I continued, "made his own big mistake and tried to run from it. He ran so much that life had no more joy."

This was what Ike had guessed during our talk in the storage shed. Because by then Ike and I knew what I was about to tell Dad.

"His own big mistake?" Dad said.

I nodded. "Dad, all those years ago, it wasn't you behind the steering wheel. It was Ted."

"Not me? But what..."

"Ted was driving," I said. "He knew you'd had so much to drink that you might not remember even getting into the car. And the car accident knocked you out. But not Ted. He pulled you over from the passenger side and put you behind the steering wheel. Then he got in on the passenger side and pretended to be unconscious. When the police got there, he let you take the blame."

Dad finally understood. As he realized what it all meant, that he no longer had to carry the guilt for what had happened, the

163

muscles around his eyes and mouth began to tremble.

He looked at me and tried to smile.

But he couldn't.

I watched the tears run down his cheeks.

chapter twenty-five

With the news of Ted Bothwell's arrest, Coach Buckley resigned. Coach knew if he didn't, he would be fired for taking a bribe from Ted to cut me from the team. So, as my bruised knuckle healed, the Titans picked up the season with a new head coach. My dad.

Dad made a great coach. He knew about basketball because he had played it himself. More importantly, something about being in jail had changed him. He was able to accept other people's mistakes better. My guess was that two things had happened. Because he no longer had to face the guilt of the past, he could be easier on himself. And his time in jail had taught him that he couldn't control everything in life. Now he was more accepting of the good and the bad things that happened around him.

So he coached us, asking us to do our best, but smiling when we made mistakes and yelling encouragement. We played without fear of failure, which is the best way to do anything.

At the end of the season, we had a shot at the state championship, which was good news. But even better was the fact that Mom was out of the hospital and in the stands as we played the game that could clinch our spot in the play-offs.

From center court, I picked her out easily in the huge crowd. She was in the stands, halfway up, behind our bench. With her dark hair pulled back, and a big pretty smile on her face, she looked like her high school photos. Anyone seeing her would have a hard time guessing that a car accident had almost killed her. Except for the cane she used when she walked, she had completely recovered. Doc Tremblay said that in less than a month she would be able to get rid of the cane.

Dad was at the bench, wearing jeans and a golf T-shirt, looking relaxed. That was good. If he was relaxed, the team was relaxed. And we needed that. We were playing the Cougars, from a high school in Indianapolis, and nobody expected us to win.

But somehow, we kept it close. Every time they scored, we came right down the court and found a way to make a basket. Tip-ins, long shots, rebounds. We did whatever it took.

My own game felt great. By the time we reached the fourth quarter, I'd ripped their defenders a dozen times. I worked on spins, fake spins, pump fakes and up-and-unders, moving and moving and moving. When my defender finally committed one way, I would break to the other, finishing with fadeaway jumpers, short jump hooks or an occasional dunk.

As the lights on the electronic scoreboard showed the clock ticking down on the fourth quarter, the noise in the gym pounded louder and louder. With less than a minute to go, we were on the losing end of a 79–78 score. The good news was we had the ball.

We moved the ball slowly down the court. To everyone, it was obvious what we wanted to do. Run the clock down and shoot in the final few seconds. If we sank our basket, the Cougars wouldn't have enough time to get back up the court and score. If we missed the basket, we'd have to take our chances on getting the rebound.

The roaring of the crowd made it impossible for us to talk to each other. It didn't matter. We knew the play. We were going to pass it around the outside until the final ten seconds. The ball would come to me and I would drive for a lay-up.

Was I scared?

Yes.

But like Dad had told us again and again during practice, all we could do was try our best. The results were far less important than the effort.

And I was ready to do my best. After all the hours of practice, all the running drills, all the shooting drills, there was nothing more I could have done to prepare for this final ten seconds.

I took the pass. Five Cougars blocked my way to the basket.

I fake-pumped like I was going for a shot from the top of the circle. It drew one of their defenders into the air. I ducked my shoulder and dribbled around him.

I wasn't thinking now. I was letting my body play. I half spun one way, spun back the other, jumped and faded back to shoot. As the ball left my hand, another defender slapped my arm.

I watched with horror as the ball hit the rim and shot sideways.

I'd missed. No time left on the clock. And I'd missed.

I had been so focused on the shot that

it took me a second to realize everyone had stopped moving. The ref had blown his whistle.

It took another second for it to sink in. He'd called a foul.

The Cougars were ahead 79-78, and I had two free throws. Sink one and we tied, forcing overtime. Sink both and we won.

Players lined both sides of the key.

I took the ball from the referee.

Cougar fans behind the basket waved their arms and yelled, trying to distract me. They thought I would choke with the play-offs on the line.

What they didn't know, though, was that I had faced a far more important free throw months earlier. The throw from the storage shed.

We'd had only one chance at starting the fire to bring us rescue. Ike Bothwell had cut a small piece off the top of the basketball. Then we'd stuffed it with rags and poured lawn mower oil on them. He'd lit the rags so they burned like a long-lasting torch. And, like a referee at the free-throw line, he had handed me the basketball, flames and oily smoke rising from the opening.

All I had was the one shot. Standing on my tiptoes on top of the box beneath the window, I aimed through the opening. My target was the Blazer's open sunroof, barely wider than a basket. And the Blazer was at least thirty feet away. If I missed, Ike and I might be stuck in the storage shed so long that we could die of thirst. And Ted would surely have escaped with the money my dad had been accused of stealing.

Worse, I had to make the shot with my left hand because of the splint on my right. I was glad I'd blown off some anger at Tom's house, practicing with my off hand.

Was it pressure? Does McDonald's have a goofy clown?

No other free throw would seem frightening after that. The burning basketball had left my fingertips, spinning too quickly for the rags to fall out. It had landed dead center in the open sunroof, falling onto the leather seats inside. Within minutes, the fire had spread, sending thick black smoke high into the sky. And not too much later, we'd heard the sound of sirens. The sound of freedom.

Knowing I had made that shot, the most important one of my life, I relaxed. This was just a game, just two simple free throws to get us into the play-offs.

My first shot went up, and while it was in the air, a hush fell over the gym. The ball came down. It hit the rim. It bounced up. Fell again. Hit the rim again. Wobbled on the edge. Circled the rim. And finally fell through.

Tie game!

Cheers roared through the gym.

The referee handed me the ball for my second free throw.

I focused on the basket. I hefted the ball and went into motion. As the basketball left my fingertips, I knew it was good. And it was. Nothing but net.

The noise in the gym somehow grew even louder. Players from the bench swarmed the court. People from the stands flooded the gym floor.

I saw my mom on her feet, clapping and yelling.

I saw my dad trying to make his way through the crowd in front of him.

Sweat rolled down my face. I felt my shoulders relax as all the tension left me. My smile started deep in my toes.

Dad finally reached me, and he put his arm around my shoulders.

"Great shot," he yelled over the crowd.

"Thanks, Dad," I said. It still took some getting used to, hearing him give me praise.

He hugged me, then he stepped back and smiled.

"And by the way," he said, "we never talk about our feelings, but I wanted you to know I love you."

Sigmund Brouwer is the best-selling author of many books for children and young adults. He has contributed to the Orca Currents series (*Wired*, *Sewer Rats*) and the Orca Sports series.

Sigmund enjoys visiting schools to talk about his books. Interested teachers can find out more by e-mailing authorbookings@coolreading.com.